I0677130

ORDER

Treesong

Cranncheol Publishing

ORDER

Published by Cranncheol Publishing.

Print Edition ISBN: 978-0-578-59282-4

Cover art by:
SelfPubBookCovers.com/RLSather

*This book is dedicated
to everyone who has taken action
in response to anthropogenic global warming
and to the future generations
of human and non-human life
who will inherit the world
created by our choices.*

ACKNOWLEDGEMENTS

Thank you to my wife, Grace, for all of your help and support during the long journey that this novel took from concept to publication. You served as my chief beta reader, my editor, my angel investor, and my loving and supportive partner. And you did it all while you were already busy excelling as a remarkable teacher and mother. Thank you.

Thank you to my daughter, Bedelia, for renewing my inspiration to write and publish climate fiction. I was already an advocate for climate justice before you were born, but your bright presence in my life has made the climate crisis feel even more real and personal. You, your friends, and your whole generation all deserve to grow and flourish in a wonderful world. That thought keeps inspiring me to write and to act, even when it seems impossible. Giving up and doing nothing is not an option. You all deserve better.

Thank you to my Patreon backers for your support throughout the writing and publication of this novel. You are few in number (so far!), but powerful in your effect on my motivation and inspiration. There were times when that monthly Patreon chapter deadline was the main driving force behind my effort to complete a chapter on time. You definitely helped make this novel possible.

Last, but certainly not least, thank you to my fellow cli-fi authors, cli-fi readers, climate communicators, and the many climate scientists, climate policy wonks, youth climate activists, climate justice advocates, climate rebels, climate educators, climate artists, climate musicians, climate game designers, and others who are all doing your part to respond to the climate crisis. May your efforts be successful, and may we somehow find our way to climate justice together.

CHAPTER 1

"Ladies and gentlemen, the fate of the world is in your hands."

Fuller Auditorium was filled to capacity with a thousand young adults in black graduation robes. Fifty-foot marble columns rose along the round edges of the auditorium. Each space between the columns featured an alcove that boasted a larger-than-life statue of a different historical figure. The ceiling was a geodesic dome composed of glowing white triangular tiles that filled the room with a warm, natural light reminiscent of sunshine. The stage was finished hardwood, a dark wenge floor adorned with intricately carved trim and bright red velvet curtains. Several dozen older adults in black robes with various academic regalia sat on stage in hefty wooden chairs. At the center of the stage stood a man in a similar robe with a golden academic hood and a large white "O" embroidered in the center of the chest.

Doctor Truman Stuart was a man in his early thirties with short black hair, sharp blue eyes, pale skin, and a muscular build mostly hidden beneath his crisp black robe. As he looked out at the audience full of young faces, his eyes shone with an intensity that stood out against his otherwise disciplined features.

"When I say that the fate of the world is in your hands, I'm not indulging in the usual fawning hyperbole of so many commencement addresses. As Initiates of Order, you are now the architects and executives of this fate. Yours are the eyes and minds that will see and grasp the many lessons of history, complexities of the contemporary world, and potential futures of the human species. Yours are the hearts that will shine most brightly with the love of humanity and grapple most intimately with the world's demons. Yours are the hands that will take every action to serve the preservation and advancement of humanity by any means necessary. Most of all, yours is the example and ideal that all of humanity may someday aspire to achieve."

Truman paused, scanning the faces of the assembled graduates. They were almost all in their very early twenties, with a few dozen older and a handful in their late teens. He could still remember sitting in the same auditorium just over a decade ago. This graduating class was somewhat more diverse than his own, with a very even gender balance and people of non-European descent making up almost half of the population. Virtually all, however, were young, able-bodied, athletic, and exceptionally intelligent.

"Since before the dawn of written history, Order has been the guiding force behind the evolution of the human species. The institution now known as Order has existed in its current form for only a few centuries. But its direct predecessors, as well as the mission and spirit of Order, extend back into prehistory."

As Truman spoke, the doors at the back and sides of the auditorium burst open. Soldiers in black body armor rushed into the room. Murmurs of concern spread through the auditorium and many of the graduates rose to their feet. Truman reflexively lowered his hands to his sides, preparing to draw two concealed weapons and dodge incoming fire if necessary. His voice, however, remained steady as he finished his sentence and started another.

"Excuse me, graduates. We have an unusual situation here."

Truman studied the soldiers who were rapidly filling the aisles of the auditorium. The first dozen in the room who were now approaching the stage had diamond-shaped white insignias on their chests.

"I'm sure that our colleagues here have a perfectly good —"

"Truman Stuart?"

As the closest soldier spoke to Truman, several others formed a wide protective circle around the two men.

"Yes. And you are?"

"A servant of Order. Tungsten Malachite Soluble Tesseract 30926."

Truman's eyes widened. The first two words were the personal code words given to him by the Guardian of Order. The second two words meant that the leadership structure of Order had been compromised. The numbers were a verification code. After standing in stunned silence for a moment, Truman spoke the appropriate countersign.

"Firmament Troglodyte Carico Hopscotch 00502."

The soldier who had spoken the coded message grabbed Truman by the arm and started leading him off the stage. The protective detail followed them closely with assault rifles at low ready, warily eyeing the audience and the remaining faculty on the stage.

As Truman started down the steps, he waved and smiled at the audience.

"Everything's fine, Initiates. Read the rest of my speech online. Enjoy your bright future with Order."

The murmuring of the audience rose to a roar. One of the faculty members stepped forward to draw their attention back to the stage while the soldiers made their exit.

As Truman left the auditorium and stepped out into the cool night air, he was surprised to see a compact black helicopter and several larger black helicopters sitting in the street and parking lot adjacent to the building. All of the aircraft were already quietly idling in preparation for takeoff, their engines and rotors rendered all but silent with the help of several advanced design features. Without any further comment, the soldiers escorted Truman to the smaller helicopter. Shortly after he was on board, the craft lifted into the air, carrying him away from the auditorium and onward to his destination.

"Please state your name and rank for the record."

Truman was sitting in a ten-foot cube room with a single steel door, bright white walls, a glossy black floor, a glowing white ceiling, and a small steel desk with two steel chairs. The man sitting on the other side of the desk was William Lamont, Guardian of Order. He was a broad-shouldered man in his late thirties with short black hair, grey eyes, and pale skin with a slightly ruddy complexion. The dark grey Glen plaid suit beneath his thick black bulletproof vest suggested that he may have also been called in unexpectedly.

"Doctor Truman Stuart, Insight of Order."

"Doctor Stuart, as Insight of Order, you have received basic training in all Level 5 Roles of Order, correct?"

"Yes. Bill, what—"

The Guardian raised his hand to interrupt Truman. "Are you prepared to assume the Role of Preceptor of Order, effective immediately?"

Truman's pulse quickened. There were several possible reasons why Order might suddenly need a new Preceptor. None of them were good.

"Yes, I am prepared to assume the Role of Preceptor of Order, effective immediately."

The Guardian breathed a sigh of relief and leaned back into his chair.

"Doctor Truman Stuart, you are now the provisional Preceptor of Order. Order is restored."

Truman felt a sudden rush. Part of it was the excitement of realizing that he was now in command of the most powerful organization in the world. But part of it was something else. His mind focused into a crystal clear state of relaxed alertness, filling him with a sudden urge to understand and solve problems.

He knew his purpose -- and there was much work to do.

"Yes. Order is restored. Thank you."

For a moment, the two men sat together in silence. Truman, the Preceptor of Order, noticed that the Guardian was studying him carefully.

"I can see the change coming over you, Truman. It's subtle, but it's there. There's a different look in your eyes now. I wasn't sure if it would happen now or later."

"Both." The Preceptor took a deep breath, listening to the air flowing in and out of his body. "I'm not receiving any specific information, but I feel a definite shift in my consciousness. It's quite a rush, really. Order is calling. I feel extremely alert and ready to take on the world."

"Then let's get to work. Come with me."

The Guardian led the Preceptor down a long hall and into a steel elevator. After a rapid descent, they stepped out into a large room with a dozen steel desks, a dozen computers, and several dozen people. The people sitting at desks wore the usual blend of business casual attire, but there were also ten guards in full black body armor with assault rifles at low ready and white diamond insignias on their chests.

"Welcome to Boston Keep's Emergency Command Center. This will be your base of operations for the next few days as you make your transition into the role as Preceptor. The Diamond Shield are my staff, of course. Everyone else is yours."

"Thank you." The Preceptor scanned the faces of the people at the desks. They were all busy working at their computers, but whenever his eyes lingered on one of them, they would look back at him expectantly. "Is everyone here Level 3 or higher?"

"Yes, of course."

"Then we may speak freely?"

"Yes."

"Good. What happened to Derek? I'll admit that we weren't close, but he never struck me as—"

"Derek's dead, Truman."

The Preceptor's eyes widened. The Guardian's otherwise

stoic face faltered into a slight frown. The two men stood together in silence for a moment while the Preceptor searched for the words to respond.

"I — I'm sorry, Bill. What happened?"

"My men — my people — are confirming the details. The short story is that he was killed by a powerful Fae creature."

"Fae?" The Preceptor stared at him in disbelief. "The Fae still kill people?"

The Guardian shook his head. "This is the first confirmed case we've seen in decades. When someone wanders off into the wild for no good reason, we always suspect the Fae. But this was definitely Fae. The only good news is that it was an isolated incident. The situation is already under control."

"You're sure?"

"Yes. I've seen to it personally."

"Good. Have you had time to prepare a report?"

"Yes, but only a brief one." The Guardian pointed to a large steel desk at the other end of the room. "You can access it at your workstation. I've also granted you access to Derek's task manager so that you can get up to speed on your duties as Preceptor. The biggest priority is choosing a new Insight to fill your old position. Choosing your team and finishing construction on the new Panopticon is a close second."

"Yes, of course." The Preceptor looked around the room again, noticing that all of the other desks were occupied. "I take it you won't be staying?"

"No. I need to conduct a thorough review of our security procedures at several sites. The Diamond Shield will offer round-the-clock protection until you're formally recognized as Preceptor. In the meantime, if you have any questions, give me a call." He leaned in closer, lowering his voice. "I don't expect any more trouble, but if anything unusual happens -- anything at all -- call me immediately. You know how strange the Fae can be."

"Understood. Thank you."

The two men shook hands. As the Guardian left the room, the Preceptor walked over to his desk and cleared his throat, clasping his hands in front of his chest with a smile.

"Alright, everyone! Let me have your attention."

Everyone at the desks in the room stopped what they were doing and gave the Preceptor their full attention.

"As you've surely heard, my name is Truman Stuart. I'm the new Preceptor of Order. Our time together in this space will be brief but fruitful. Please continue with your current tasks until otherwise directed. If anything urgent comes up, please bring it to my attention. In the meantime, I have some catching up to do."

He started to sit down, then stopped for a moment, raising his index finger.

"Also, from this point forward, I expect everyone who is not Level 5 to refer to me by my proper title, Preceptor. While I encourage an informal and collaborative work environment, let's not forget who we are. I am the Preceptor of Order, and you are among the most advanced Initiates of Order. Together, we will create a better world."

Most of the people at the desks nodded in agreement. The Preceptor nodded along with them and sat down at his new desk. After entering several passwords, he opened the Guardian's report and the previous Preceptor's task manager.

There was much work to do.

CHAPTER 2

Providence Catalysis was a colonial-era mansion standing alone in a circular clearing on a peak in the Appalachian Mountains. The red brick building consisted of a large two-story central block with connecting hallways leading to two additional wings with slightly rounded facades that were each half as large as the main structure. The building had numerous mirrored bulletproof windows, a white roof and columns, a meticulously trimmed topiary garden featuring numerous elaborate abstract shapes, and four life-sized marble archangel statues. The archangels were kneeling on either side of the cobblestone path leading up to the front door, their hands clasped in prayer and their heads bowed in deference to those who passed between them.

The Preceptor emerged from a nearly silent black helicopter idling on a cobblestone helipad near the main entrance to the building. He was wearing a tailored wool and silk black suit and a golden sash with a bold embroidered black "O" with a white center. As soon as he and his four blackclad Diamond Shield bodyguards had their feet on the ground, the helicopter took off, joining several others in the clear blue sky overhead. The small swarm of uncannily quiet aircraft scattered in seemingly random directions, with a few descending toward the base of the mountain while the others ascended and sped off to sights unseen.

This was only the second time that the Preceptor had visited Providence Catalysis. He walked down the cobblestone path slowly, pausing to admire the archangel statues.

"Raphael. Gabriel. Michael. Auriel." He paused, turning to

address one of the bodyguards. "Asim, is it?"

"Yes, sir."

"Tell me, Asim." He waved his hand in the direction of the archangels. "These four represent tremendous power. They embody the four archetypal powers of Order. Why are they kneeling?"

Asim studied the statues carefully, examining their servile posture and peaceful expressions.

"Because they serve Order."

"Yes. Excellent answer. Because they serve Order." He took a few steps toward the nearest statue, touching the clasped hands with his fingertips. "But it's more than that. See how the eyes look directly at the middle of the path, the spot where our feet meet the ground. They know that we are living embodiments of Order. The sight of our presence in the world comforts them. Their power is at our service -- but only as long as we continue to walk the path of Order. Do you understand?"

Asim nodded in agreement. "Yes, sir."

"Good. On days like this, it's important to remember why we're all here."

The Preceptor and his bodyguards walked up to the main entrance of the building. As they approached, the door swung open and an attendant in a white tuxedo welcomed them inside.

Deep inside the mountain below the colonial-era mansion, there was a massive hidden Cold War era bunker. The Preceptor had been there once before to receive his initiation as Insight of Order. Now, he had returned for his initiation as Preceptor of Order.

The preparation for the ceremony was very similar. There was the long ride down the slow-moving freight elevator; the long walk alone down the cold concrete corridor; the ten-foot cube room where his ceremonial garb was waiting for him.

Surprisingly, the garb of the Preceptor initiation was fairly simple: a white knee-length tabard with gold trim and a large black "O" on the chest, along with a simple black belt with a gold buckle and trim. He wore the tabard over his suit, waited for the sound of the bell, and proceeded into the next room.

The Inner Temple of Order was a large round room with a smooth marble floor and domed marble ceiling. Both were made entirely of the same distinctive Yule Marble as the Lincoln Memorial and the Tomb of the Unknowns. There was also a large marble altar at the center of the room. As expected, there were only thirteen other people present.

The Council of Order sat in thirteen golden thrones arranged in a semicircle facing the heavy oak doors at the entrance to the room. They were dressed in ornate black robes adorned with various sashes, hoods, cords, and medallions. For security reasons, they were almost never in the same physical location at the same time. The only exception to this rule was for Level 5 initiations and Council initiations.

As the Preceptor walked down the red carpet and approached the altar, the Councillors studied him in silence. When he reached the end of the carpet, he fell to one knee, bowed his head, and awaited the approach of the Sovereign of Order.

The Sovereign of Order rose from his seat at the center of the Council. Percival Sword was a man of modest stature but powerful presence. Even amidst all of the reverent architecture and ceremonial regalia, he instantly commanded the attention of everyone in the room. His brilliant blue eyes twinkled like twin sapphires above his sharp Roman nose and broad thin-lipped smile. He wore a solid diamond crown emblazoned with a large diamond Eye of Providence framed in a gold circle over the center of his forehead.

As the Sovereign strode forward to the altar, all eyes were upon him. The usual long-winded recitations at the beginning of all formal Order ceremonies had already been taken care of before the Preceptor's entrance, so the Sovereign proceeded with the main action of the ceremony.

"Welcome, Initiate of Order. Rise and tell us your name."

The Preceptor rose to his feet.

"My name is Truman Stuart."

"Welcome, Truman Stuart. As an Initiate of Order, what is your oath?"

Truman had spoken the words of the oath so many times that they had become as natural as breathing. As he spoke them now in the presence of the Council, however, it was not an act of rote repetition. It was a heartfelt affirmation of his innate sense of duty in his service to Order.

"I am a servant of Order. My feet walk the path of Order. My hands do the work of Order. My words speak the truth of Order. My heart loves the good of Order. I am Order become flesh, flesh become Order, the living victory of Order in a world that would be lost without it."

The Sovereign nodded approvingly.

"Truly, you are a servant of Order. Tell me, Initiate. Are you trained in the ways of the First Level of Order?"

"Yes, Sovereign. I wield the coin inscribed with the pentacle of Order."

"Are you trained in the ways of the Second Level of Order?"

"Yes, Sovereign. I wield the wand of action in the service of Order."

"Are you trained in the ways of the Third Level of Order?"

"Yes, Sovereign. I wield the chalice that holds the waters of Order."

"Are you trained in the ways of the Fourth Level of Order?"

"Yes, Sovereign. I wield the sword that cleaves the way to Order."

"Are you trained in the ways of the Fifth Level of Order?"

"Yes, Sovereign. I wear the crown that guides the path of Order."

"Truly, you are a crown servant of Order." The Sovereign took a step forward, placing his hands on the altar. "You have been summoned here today to assume the highest role of Order outside of the Council. As Preceptor of Order, you will be personally responsible for overseeing the development of this entire world. The Council is tasked with developing a broad vision for the present and future Order of humanity and the world it inhabits. You as the Preceptor will be tasked with clarifying that vision into specific courses of action that make this Order manifest in the world. You must guide and teach all Initiates of Order, just as Order guides and teaches all of humanity. Do you understand your duty as Preceptor of Order?"

"Yes, Sovereign. I understand my duty."

"Do you swear to place this duty above all others?"

"I swear to place my duty as Preceptor of Order above all other duties. I will guide and teach the Initiates of Order. Together, we will make Order manifest in this world."

"Very well. Initiate, kneel before the Altar of Order."

The Preceptor fell to one knee, bowing his head before the altar. The Sovereign reached down onto the altar and picked up a golden crown. The crown was similar to his own except that the headband was made of gold rather than diamond. It featured the same diamond Eye of Providence framed in a gold circle. He raised the crown aloft for a moment, then walked around the altar to stand within reach of the Preceptor.

"As Sovereign of Order, I hereby bestow upon you the role of Preceptor of Order. You will serve as Preceptor for the rest of your natural life or until such a time as the Council deems it necessary to choose a new Preceptor. All of Order will answer to you, and you will answer to me. Together, we will create a better world."

The Sovereign placed the golden crown on the Preceptor's head.

As soon as he felt the weight of the crown, the Preceptor experienced a sudden rush of information and sensation. His mind focused into a crystal clarity unlike anything he had ever experienced. It occurred to him that a better world really was possible. This was no longer just an abstract thought. Various aspects of Order's operations and plans came to mind in great detail. Some of this information was familiar, but much of it was new. It was like watching the teeth of many crystal gears interlocking and spinning around each other with clockwork precision. He realized that when seen from the proper perspective, all the world was an incredibly large and complex puzzle waiting to be solved. A magnificent new world was possible. Most of the pieces were already in play. All that remained was to bring them all together in the right order.

The Sovereign waited a few moments while the Preceptor processed this new information. Eventually, he spoke.

"Rise now, Preceptor of Order, and fulfill your duty."

The Preceptor rose to his feet. His mind still had access to all of that detailed information flowing from the governing consciousness of Order. But with effort, he was able to return his attention to the information of his senses and his ordinary waking consciousness. Even so, he remained in a state of relaxed alertness that went beyond his usual calm discipline. Now more than ever, he knew who he was. He knew his purpose, and he knew how to serve that purpose.

He was the Preceptor of Order -- and he was ready to create a better world.

CHAPTER 3

The Preceptor stepped out of the elevator and into the newly completed command center of Order.

The Panopticon was a spherical room with a hundred foot diameter. The bottom half of the sphere was filled with a series of multicolored transparent ceramic desks of various shapes and sizes. Several dozen men and women in business casual attire were stocking these desks with flat screen monitors, office supplies, and occasional personal items such as family photos, paintings, potted plants, and small sculptures. The curved blue dome of the upper half of the room was framed with two tiers of transparent aluminum walkways holding additional desks that were also in the process of being set up for use. A lone walkway extended out to the center of the room to support a six foot diameter crystal sphere. A stout man in a white lab coat was standing next to the sphere, alternately tapping on his tablet and speaking with emphatic gestures to a smaller man in cobalt blue overalls.

For a moment, the Preceptor slowed to a stop, quietly observing the hustle and bustle of activity throughout the room. All of the faces were familiar, but a few he had only seen on a monitor up until this point. They were all so intent on their various tasks that none had noticed his arrival. He nodded approvingly and approached the man in white.

Dr. Katsutoshi Alessandro Aino was a middle-aged man with scruffy black hair, lively brown eyes, and a well-groomed moustache. He wore an expensive Italian suit beneath a simple cotton lab coat. He was thoroughly immersed in his work with his assistant until he noticed the Preceptor approaching.

"Ah, Preceptor! Buongiorno! Ohayou gozaimasu!" He slid his tablet into the pocket of his lab coat and shook the Preceptor's hand vigorously. "Welcome to the Panopticon, my friend! What do you think? It's better than the old offices, yes?"

The Preceptor took another careful look around the room. "Very good, Katsutoshi. I like the new interactive walls and natural spectrum lighting. How's the Eye doing?"

"The Eye is good, Preceptor. Molto bene." He patted the large crystal sphere affectionately. "It's already up and running. We're just adjusting the wireless communication with your little crystal ball here. You share my flair for the dramatic, yes? A crystal ball as tall as a person?"

"The Eye is one of the greatest modern achievements of Order, Katsutoshi. Interacting with it on a standard issue flat screen simply wouldn't do."

"Indeed, indeed." He pulled his tablet out of his pocket and turned to his assistant. "The servers must be ready by now, Ernesto. Turn on the power."

The man in the blue jumpsuit reached down to press a small clear button that blended almost seamlessly into the walkway at the base of the crystal sphere. After a few moments, the sphere sprang to life, filling with a bright white light that soon transformed into a complex full color display.

The Eye of Order displayed a map of the world. Most of the oceans were a pale greenish grey while the land masses were complex blends of various hues, tints, shades, and tones of green, yellow, orange, and red. Most of the land was dominated by various shades of green. Major cities were criss-crossed with patches of green, yellow, and orange. Several whole nations were more yellow and orange than the rest of the map. Each continent had hundreds of small splotches of red scattered across its face like so many blemishes.

The Preceptor immediately recognized the data that the Eye was presenting through this colorful globe. During his tenure as Insight of Order, he had overseen the ongoing development of many different models of the world. Each model represented a different discipline's perspective on a particular problem or a particular aspect of human society and life on Earth. Now, all of these models had been quantified and synthesized into a single metamodel capable of tracking the current integrity of consensus reality and running projections for the future stability and development of Order.

As the Preceptor stared at the Eye, he touched his golden crown with two fingers near his right temple and studied the globe. The room gradually fell silent as everyone noticed what was happening. For a long time, he ignored them, instead paying close attention to the Eye. Each splotch of red or stretch of yellow and orange represented some known problem -- a pocket of Anomalous activity in need of correction. Many of the marks were easily identifiable: wars and civil unrest on several continents; another record-breaking typhoon in southeast Asia; rogue Anomalous Revolution cells wreaking havoc in Guangdong. Others were not as obvious, but he knew that he could access more information on his tablet.

After staring at the Eye for a minute or two, he took a few steps back and faced as many people as he could given the spherical shape of the room.

"Initiates of Order, I present to you the Eye of Order!"

Everyone burst into applause. The Preceptor bowed slightly to everyone in the room, then bowed more deeply to Dr. Aino.

"Thank you, Dr. Aino, for all of your hard work on this project."

"My pleasure, Preceptor. Now go and have some fun with your new toy. If you need me, you know where to find me. Come, Ernesto, let's be on our way."

Dr. Aino and Ernesto walked to the elevator. The Preceptor walked slowly around the Eye, examining the coloration of each city, each region, and each continent. When he had completed his circle, he pulled a tablet out of one of the pockets of his cargo pants and opened his connection to the Eye.

It was time to start studying all of that beautiful data.

◆ ◆ ◆

The Panopticon was mostly quiet during the first grave-yard shift. All of the colorful desks had been fully stocked and decorated with personal effects. Everyone currently on duty was studying the data on their computers, frequently tapping and swiping their screens or typing in new information on wireless keyboards. For several hours, the Preceptor was the most quiet of all, typing little and barely moving as he examined the finer details of the various models and the remarkably complex metamodel. He occasionally glanced at the Eye to compare the display on the crystal sphere and the display on his screen.

Only a few weeks ago, as the Insight of Order, he had helped coordinate the effort to quantify and synthesize these models into a single metamodel. Now, as he studied the results of the year-long effort, the expression on his face slowly soured.

"Something isn't right here."

The Preceptor grabbed his tablet, striding across the short distance between his cobalt blue desk and the Eye. With a few taps and swipes on his tablet, he opened the control panel for the Eye and chose a new projection.

Model: Meta. Scenario: Standard. Duration: 100 years.

The Eye faded to white briefly, then displayed a colorful globe map very similar to the one it had just been displaying. The only obvious difference was that there was a counter at the equator displaying the current year. As the counter started advancing through the years, the colors on the globe fluctuated smoothly. After a couple of decades, the fluctuations became more sporadic. Around 2050, the entire globe flashed crimson and quickly faded to black.

"That can't be right."

The Preceptor adjusted the settings.

Model: Meta. Scenario: Favorable. Duration: 100 years.

The Eye faded to white again, then displayed a colorful globe. For the first decade, the colors shifted more toward green, with most of the world becoming the nice bright green that indicated a very strong and healthy presence of Order. Around 2050, the entire globe rapidly deteriorated, gradually fading to black in the late 2050s.

The Preceptor glared at the Eye. He looked down at his tablet to make sure that there wasn't a discrepancy between the two displays. The smaller display showed the exact same information as the large crystal sphere.

Even under favorable conditions -- with every uncertainty resolved in Order's favor -- the metamodel still indicated a total collapse of Order sometime in the late 2050s. No nation would be unaffected. No nation would be left standing. If there were any human survivors at all, they would live in circumstances so far removed from the current reality that it was difficult to predict and impossible to control.

By this point, the dozen other people left in the Panopticon for the graveyard shift had stopped working and started watching the Eye. The Preceptor ran the favorable projection again with similar results. For a moment, he simply glared at the Eye in anger and disbelief, his free hand clenching tightly at his side. When he remembered that he was surrounded by a dozen key staff, he made a conscious effort to transform his emotions, flipping the anger into exuberance.

"Attention everyone! I need all eyes on this problem. The metamodel is telling me that Order will collapse in the 2050s. Is this a flaw in the model or is this the reality we're facing? Give me your best guess in five minutes or less. Go!"

Everyone else in the room scrambled back to their desks. As they tapped, swiped, and talked their way through the data and the models, the Preceptor decided to run a few more scenarios.

There were hundreds of preset scenarios. He had worked directly on a few of them, but most were the products of his staff. The Global Depression scenario. The Global Abundance scenario. The Generic Epidemic scenario. The Genetic Modification scenario. The various World War III scenarios. The details

ORDER

varied, but the world always faded to black in a matter of decades. Every time it did, the Preceptor felt something churn in his stomach.

This wasn't an error. He didn't even have to look at his tablet anymore to confirm that it wasn't an error. As he cleared his mind, he felt a flood of information from his intuitive connection as Preceptor of Order. The details were a bit much to take in at once, but the overall picture was clear.

This was real.

As the Preceptor returned his attention to the present moment and the various scenarios playing out in front of him, he noticed one of his newest staff members approaching the Eye.

Dr. Cassandra Bharati was a woman in her mid thirties with bright brown eyes, dark tan skin, a crisp white lab coat over a yellow silk dress, and long black hair drawn back into a high ponytail. She approached the Preceptor slowly and quietly, showing due deference without a hint of timidity or hesitation.

"I know the problem, Preceptor."

"Oh?" The Preceptor's clenched fist loosened a bit. "I'm curious to hear your take on it. Your focus is on earth sciences, correct?"

"Yes." She pulled her tablet out of her lab coat pocket, scrolling through a long list of scenarios. "Run the Impossibly Good Climate scenario."

The Preceptor looked down at his own tablet, scrolling through the list to select the proper scenario.

Model: Meta. Scenario: Impossibly Good Climate (Counterfactual). Duration: 100 years.

The Eye faded to white briefly, then displayed a colorful globe map very similar to the present day map. As it advanced through the decades, the colors fluctuated significantly, with some areas turning green while others turned red. The overall color balance, however, remained fairly steady. At the end of the 100 year simulation, most of the globe was still green.

The Preceptor studied the Eye carefully. He ran his fingers along the cool crystal surface, touching the various shades of red, orange, yellow, and green. As the information slowly sank in, he lowered his hand again, clenching it tightly at his side.

"Climate? You're telling me that climate change leads to the collapse of Order in all of the other scenarios?"

"Yes, Preceptor."

"And this is valid? Not an error in the data or the model?"

"Yes, Preceptor. The global climate is currently undergoing catastrophic changes due to anthropogenic global warming. These changes are more than enough to destabilize global society by mid-century. This is an existential threat."

The Preceptor glared at the Eye. Somehow, the bright colors of the impossibly favorable climate scenario seemed to be mocking him. Scrolling through the list of scenarios, he found a relevant one that he hadn't tried yet.

Model: Meta. Scenario: Geoengineering For Climate Stabilization. Duration: 100 Years.

The Eye faded to white briefly, then displayed a colorful globe map very similar to the present day map. As it advanced through the decades, the colors briefly brightened, then rapidly faded to red and black in the 2050s.

The Preceptor pounded on the Eye. The sudden sting that he felt in the edge of his hand was oddly comforting. He pounded on the Eye three more times in rapid succession before regaining his composure, transforming his frustration into enthusiasm.

"Mystery solved! Dr. Bharati, I need all top ranking science personnel in the main conference room in ten minutes. If they're asleep, wake them up. I'll contact a few other Level 4s. We need to discuss these results."

"Yes, Preceptor."

Dr. Bharati bowed slightly before hurrying back to her desk. The Preceptor tapped on his tablet, returning the Eye to a display of the present day map. As he stared at the various splotches of red, he envisioned them slowly expanding, swallowing up the world with all of the chaos and violence that they represented.

There wasn't any time to lose.

◆ ◆ ◆

The conference room was twenty feet wide by forty feet long. The transparent ceramic walls and ceiling were usually white or sky blue, but today they had been set to display a live panoramic view of a meadow in the foothills of the Swiss Alps. At a glance, the appearance of being outdoors was convincing, though careful examine by a keen eye would reveal the illusion.

The clear oblong table at the center of the room was covered with stray tablets, notepads filled with lined legal paper, and a few tidy stacks of empty food trays and tall drinking glasses. Several trays at the edges of the table still had leftover bits of food that had been forgotten at some point during the fourteen hour marathon brainstorming session: pizza crusts, cake crumbs, a half-eaten sandwich, a few forkfuls of stir fry, and other odds and ends, all sitting within easy reach but not recently touched. The Preceptor, Dr. Aino, Dr. Bharati, and ten other members of the Preceptor's staff sat around the table, deeply immersed in a combination of hushed conversation, tapping and swiping on tablets, and scribbling on notepads.

The Preceptor pushed away his tablet and sighed, standing for a moment to do a few quick stretches. He had already been up for fifteen hours when this session had started, so he wasn't at his peak alertness. Something told him that they would have a breakthrough soon, though, so he kept pushing himself and his staff to continue.

"Dr. Aino. You've been very quiet for a long time now. It's unlike you." A few people around the table laughed, including Dr. Aino. "Any news? Are you working on something specific?"

"Yes, Preceptor, yes." He continued typing on a virtual keyboard projected by his tablet. "It's a very complex and unusual model. It will need some refinement later, but the first edition is almost complete. Two minutes, perhaps. I will put it on the screen when it's ready."

"Good. Thank you, Toshi."

The Preceptor picked up his tablet and spent several minutes reviewing other reports unrelated to the metamodel that required his attention. When the wall across the room from him went blank, he set aside his tablet and looked at Dr. Aino's model.

Model: Meta. Scenario: Favorable Anomalies. Duration: 100 years. Loop: 100.

A large colorful globe appeared on the wall. The projection looped through the same scenario 100 times in less than a minute. Some of the scenarios ended in a world that faded to black, but the rest ended in a mostly green-yellow-orange world. At the end, it displayed a brief summary of the results.

Survival: 79/100. Progress: 68/100. Confidence. 93%.

"Excellent." The Preceptor smiled, clasping his hands together in front of his chest. "It's not ideal, but I'll take it. No counterfactuals?"

"No counterfactuals, Preceptor."

"How does it work?"

"It's hard to explain in words, you see." Dr. Aino displayed some of the technical details of the projection on the wall. "I had to modify the constraints we were placing on the system. We usually seek to contain the Anomalous. If it is an anomalous person, we may detain them. If it is anomalous technology, we suppress or delay it. If it is some anomalous natural phenomenon, we either learn from it or manage it. You see what I'm saying?"

"Yes, yes. Control and reduce all Anomalous phenomena. This is a Level 1 concept. This is a core component of our mission."

"Yes, Preceptor. But none of our solutions seemed to be working. So I asked myself something. What would it be like to let a little bit of the chaos back in? Very selectively, you see.

Strategically. Introduce some strange elements into the system that can do things beyond our power. These elements would create certain specific changes to the culture, the economy, the ecology, that our models currently deem impossible in the allotted time frame. This is the basis of my model."

By this point, all eyes in the room were on Dr. Aino and the Preceptor. The Preceptor studied the details of the model carefully, using his tablet to scroll through various subsets of information. On the surface, the very premise seemed impossibly dangerous. But the results of the model were clear. The longer he looked at the model, the more he felt a rush of additional information confirming the potential success of this course of action.

"This makes sense. It's dangerous, but not as dangerous as inaction. As much as I hate to say it, this may be what we're looking for." He set down his tablet, mustering a broad and bright-eyed smile as he addressed the rest of his staff. "Thank you everyone for your cooperation! You can keep working if you like, or you can go off duty whenever you're ready. Please update your respective teams about this new model. Until something better comes along, this model is our top priority. I also want a summary of our best geoengineering options in my inbox in twelve hours. Meeting adjourned."

Everyone else in the room breathed a sigh of relief. Several people gathered their belongings and scurried out of the room. Dr. Aino and Dr. Bharati started talking to each other and comparing their notes. The Preceptor rubbed his bleary eyes, picked up his tablet, and sat down at the table. He still had to respond to a few messages he had received during the meeting. After that, though, he knew he had to catch up on sleep.

He had his work cut out for him.

CHAPTER 4

"I don't like it."

The Preceptor sat alone in a ten-foot cube telepresence room. He was sitting at a small metal desk facing the wall opposite the door. The other walls were set to display mahogany panelling, but the wall he was facing featured a two-way live feed connected to a similar room in a distant building. In this room, the Guardian was sitting behind a similar desk giving the Preceptor an incredulous look.

"I don't like it either, Bill. But it makes sense. We can't make the necessary changes to our energy infrastructure and economy quickly enough. If we rapidly reduce fossil fuel consumption to zero, society collapses. If we conduct a massive geoengineering campaign to counteract the effects of climate change, there's about a 99% chance that it'll backfire and start World War III. What we need is a wild card -- something that can alter the system parameters in a way that we can't."

"That all sounds well and good in theory, Truman. But you're not talking about theory. You're talking about reaching out to a bunch of deviants, criminals, and madmen. You're talking about handing the keys to the kingdom over to people who oppose the very existence of Order."

"Nonsense." The Preceptor flicked his hand dismissively. "Any Anomalous individuals or technology that we use in this operation will be strictly monitored. I'm well aware of the dangers of Anomalies. I used to be the Insight of Order. I know more about the Verwechseln scale than you do. Who do you think sent you all of those reports about Anomalies?"

"Again, that's theory. You're well-versed in theory. This

is practice. You haven't had to deal with Anomalies out in the field. I've seen good men lose their lives because some fanatic wanted to end civilization. I've gone head to head with people who think it's their God-given right to create fire out of thin air or move objects with their minds. There's no place in the world for these freaks, Truman. If you give them an inch, they'll take a mile. If you let them in, Order will fall."

"Order will fall if we do nothing. I'm not asking your permission, Bill. This is my call. We're doing this."

The Guardian shook his head. "You're putting me in a difficult situation, Truman. I'll follow your lead, but I still don't like it. Tell your lab geeks to keep searching for alternate solutions."

"They already are, Bill. Trust me. I don't like this any more than you do. In the meantime, this is the plan. Find Anomalous individuals and technologies that may have a positive impact on the climate crisis. I've already started compiling research and gathering intelligence. I need to know that you and your people are with me on this."

"Understood. Consider it done. In fact, I already have a recommendation."

"Oh?"

"Yes. There's someone that past Preceptors have turned to for advice about difficult situations. He's not on the books because he's too Anomalous to meet today's standards for tag and release. He's about a 7 or 8 on the Verwechseln scale."

The Preceptor gave him a curious look. "How haven't I heard about this? Who is this person?"

"You've probably heard the stories about his involvement in World War II and the Cold War. You just didn't know that he was still alive. Or real, for that matter."

The Preceptor's eyes widened. "No, it couldn't be."

"Yes, it could be. And it is."

"Bertram Muhnugin?"

"Bertram Muhnugin."

◆ ◆ ◆

Bertram Muhnugin was a legendary figure among the initiates of Order. Some said that he was an alien. Some said that he was a mutant. Some said that he was a magical creature, a living relic from the days when such Anomalies openly walked the world in broad daylight. Whatever he was, the stories said that his gift of prophecy had guided the Preceptors of Order for generations.

As the Preceptor settled into his seat on the helicopter, he examined the contents of the dog-eared black leather binder that he had found among the last Preceptor's personal effects. All of Order's official records had been digitized long ago, so he was intrigued by the prospect of paging through a physical binder full of secret information. The smell of old leather, the crinkle of yellowing paper, the slightly uneven typewritten font of the earliest pages, and the hand-written notes in the margins all gave the artifact a certain irresistible charm. As he turned each page, the Preceptor studied the words and images carefully, soaking up the meaning of a document that had been handed down to him by the most powerful men in the world.

According to the notes, some of the stories that he had heard during his early days in Order were true, or at least partially true. Bertram Muhnugin had been born in the midst of the Mexican-American war in 1847 or 1848. He was believed to be a Theological Anomaly, or what past Preceptors had called a Demigod or Godling. He was more or less human, but at some point in his family history, some highly Anomalous and little-understood event had permanently altered the DNA of all future generations. The file included references to his unusual appearance and apparent lack of aging, but the most important documented Anomaly was something rare and elusive that no one in Order fully understood.

Bertram Muhnugin had the ability to see the future.

As the Preceptor read and reread the document, the

helicopter eventually reached its destination. He set down the binder, waited for the helicopter door to open, and stepped out into the night.

The Preceptor found himself in an empty field of tangled weeds. He was staring at a moonlit house that loomed at the top of a hill surrounded by dense woods. The house itself was surprisingly ordinary at first glance, a simple two-storey colonial with blue wood siding and black shuttered windows. However, it was built at the base of an exceptionally tall and broad yew tree that towered over and around it, creating the illusion that the house was embedded in the base of the massive tree.

A lone figure emerged from the woods, approaching the house on a narrow dirt path that weaved its way through the tangles of weeds and rose to the crown of the hill. He wore a dark blue cloak and carried a gnarled wooden staff. As he made his way up the hill, two abnormally large ravens flew over his head and circled several times before coming to rest on the lowest branches of the yew tree. Though the path was long and winding, the wandering stranger quickly made his way to the front doorstep, opening the door and stepping inside.

The Preceptor stepped slowly and carefully through the tangle of knee-high weeds. Once he reached the path, his pace quickened, only to slow again as he approached the top of the hill.

The front door had been left open.

The Preceptor stopped a few yards short of the door, studying it carefully from a distance. The entryway was dark and empty, but there was a light shining deeper inside the house. As the Preceptor stood near the doorstep, a lone voice from pierced the night.

> *"Nobody knows... the trouble I've seen.*
> *Nobody knows my sorrow.*
> *Nobody knows... the trouble I've seen.*
> *Glory... hal-le-lu-jah."*

The old house and tree hummed in resonance with the sound of the unseen voice. After listening for a long moment, the Preceptor stepped forward. The two ravens eyed him warily, croaking loudly as he stepped onto the small brick doorstep. Somehow, he felt as though the birds were peering deep into his soul, reading him like a book and croaking their response in a language he couldn't understand. But they made no motion to stop him, so he reached out to knock on the open door. Before his knuckles struck the wood, the ravens and the singing fell silent.

"You may enter, Truman."

The Preceptor's pulse quickened. He stepped into the entryway, searching for the source of the voice and the light. After passing a staircase that led both upstairs and downstairs, he turned left and found what he was looking for.

He was a tall, lean figure with ashen skin, a deep grey color that hinted at a once-bronze complexion lost in a lifeless pallor. He removed his dark blue traveling cloak to reveal a black suit, crimson shirt, black tie, and black fedora. His body was impossibly gaunt, accentuating his gangly limbs and long, hollow face. His left eye was missing, with the empty socket covered in a thin layer of scar tissue. His right eye was a sharp burst of shining silver. The two abnormally large ravens that had just been outside a moment ago were now perched behind him on a large wooden altar inscribed with runes. The altar and the bookshelves around the room were filled with tidy stacks of old books, parchments, and various tools and artifacts made of wood, stone, leather, and bone. The room was lit by a fire flickering and crackling in a brick fireplace.

As the Preceptor walked into the room, the man's lone silver eye rose to meet him. For a moment, the Preceptor stood at the edge of the room, speechless. Eventually, he looked his host in the eye and spoke.

"Bertram Muhnugin?"

The man stared at him in breathless silence for the span

of several heartbeats, looking right through him in the flickering light of the fire.

"I've been called worse. By your predecessors, no less."

"You know who I am?"

For a moment, Bertram smiled — a cold, toothy, malevolent expression bordering on a grimace. When he spoke, his face lost any trace of humor.

"You know who and what I am. How could I not know who you are? I'm not a two-bit carnival fortune teller. I know who you are. I've been waiting a long time for this day."

"This day?"

"Yes. My last conversation with a Preceptor. The thought has put me in an uncommonly good mood." Bertram pointed to two wooden chairs near the fireplace. "Please, have a seat."

The two men sat next to each other, their chairs facing the fireplace. Bertram stared into the fire, watching the flames flicker as shadows danced across his pallid skin. The Preceptor looked back and forth between the strange man and the fire, gathering his thoughts before speaking.

"I have so many questions."

"You have more questions on your mind than most of your predecessors. However, you will only ask me nine. Three of these have already been spoken. Ask me the other six before I grow weary of your presence."

The Preceptor nodded, mentally counting his questions.

"How can I avert the catastrophic effects of climate change?"

"You can't."

The Preceptor's eyes widened. "I can't?"

"The deed is done, oh great and powerful Preceptor. The deed is done."

The Preceptor looked at Bertram in stunned silence. Bertram picked up a poker and a piece of wood, stoking the fire as he continued.

"You have already seen this truth. Like a proper child of Hermes, you have made your measurements, performed your calculations, uncovered your secrets, and gathered your information from all corners of a cornerless world. Through your divination, you have seen the voracious appetite of man devouring whole continents of life. You have seen the black blood of the earth sucked from beneath the soil. You have seen the alchemists create great wonders and perform great feats by unleashing the potent energy of this necromantic brew. You have seen them spew their foul soot into the air until the perturbations of wind and water and flame threaten to tear asunder the very flesh and bone of life itself. Order has embraced these alchemists and guided these technologies into being. Now that the deed is done, Order is powerless to undo it."

The Preceptor shook his head. "But I've read the stories about you. Preceptors past have come to you for advice. You've helped Order neutralize other Anomalies that would have destroyed the world. Why not now?"

Bertram sighed, setting aside the poker and staring into the fire. "This climate crisis you seek to avert has been woven into the fabric of the world by none other than Order. For nearly two hundred years, I have studied every thread of this tapestry. Peasant and king alike stand naked before me, their every secret laid bare beneath my gaze. There are many weavers, and more still who are woven. A master weaver may alter the dance of the warp and weft with a careful hand and keen eye. I have aided past Preceptors in this subtle art when it suited my purposes. Yet I have seen none in all the world who can change what is now woven. The pattern is all but complete, and no hand can unweave it without destroying the tapestry."

For a long time, the two men sat in silence. The Preceptor stared into the fire, contemplating Bertram's words. The ravens stirred on their perches, peering at the Preceptor with restless eyes. Eventually, the Preceptor spoke.

"If Order can't solve this crisis, is there anyone who can?"

"There are those who will try. In nineteen days, you will meet a woman who will lead the effort. She is a child of the gods, a woman of change. Her light will reveal the shadows of Order.

She will be the last person who I speak to in this life. My last moments are unclear even to me, as are the days beyond them. But I know that even she does not have the power to change what is coming. No one does."

The Preceptor rose to his feet, glaring at Bertram.

"Then why bother? I didn't come here for more defeatism. I don't understand the point of any of this if there's nothing anyone can do."

Bertram's face twisted into a cold, cruel smile. "You bother because that is your strand in the tapestry, just as it is my strand to see. I can see everything that happens in every moment between the day of my birth and the day of my death. Everything. Your mind cannot grasp what I have seen. I have known for almost two hundred years that we are approaching a knot that no one can untie. My only comfort in that time has been the knowledge that I will not live to see that knot."

The Preceptor clasped his hands together in front of his chest.

"If you aren't there at the end, then you can't be certain how it ends."

"Nothing is certain, Truman. But there is not a weaver alive who can change the tapestry so forcefully in so little time without tearing it asunder. That much I know."

"We'll see." The Preceptor looked over at the ravens, then back at Bertram. "Any last words of advice for me before I go?"

"Yes. Ask the Sovereign why your predecessor chose to speak with the Fae. Now, if you'll excuse me, I have one last journey to prepare for."

Bertram rose to his feet. The Preceptor raised a hand to interrupt him.

"But--"

"You have asked your questions. My service to the Preceptors is finally at an end. Go now or I will speak truths that you're not ready to hear."

Bertram walked over to the altar and started gathering pouches and scroll cases into a leather backpack. When the ravens grew restless, he shooed them away with a wave of his hands. The Preceptor took one last look at Bertram before following the ravens out the door.

CHAPTER 5

The Preceptor sat at his cobalt blue desk in the Panopticon, staring at his screen in silence. He tapped the screen to select another scenario for review.

Dr. Aino and his team had prepared dozens of new scenarios for the Preceptor's review. Most of them were interesting variations on the term 'Anomalous': Anomalous Geoengineering; Anomalous Energy Infrastructure; Economic Anomalies; Electoral Anomalies; and more. The Preceptor was impressed with the level of detail that had gone into conceptualizing and modelling each scenario. The results varied, but they all had one thing in common: failure. So far, there was still only one scenario that reliably resulted in a high chance of survival for the human species.

Favorable Anomalies.

He ran it again just to confirm the results.

Model: Meta. Scenario: Favorable Anomalies. Duration: 100 years. Loop: 100.

A large colorful globe appeared on his screen. The projection looped through the same scenario 100 times in less than a minute. Someone had tweaked the details slightly in the past few days, but the results were essentially the same.

Survival: 77/100. Progress: 71/100. Confidence. 95%.

The Preceptor pushed away from his desk, rolling back slightly in his black leather executive chair. After glaring at the results for a while, his eyes suddenly brightened. He stood up and walked up to the large crystal sphere at the center of the Panopticon.

"Dr. Bharati, join me at the Eye for a moment."

Dr. Bharati blinked in surprise and looked up from her screen. Her desk was on the transparent walkway above the elevator at the far end of the room.

"Yes, Preceptor."

She walked down the small set of stairs and joined the Preceptor on the lone walkway that supported the Eye.

"How can I help you?"

"I have an idea, Cassandra."

He pulled out his tablet and scrolled through a list of scenarios, tapping the name of the one that he was looking for.

Model: Meta. Scenario: Impossibly Good Climate (Counterfactual). Duration: 100 years. Loop: 100.

The favorable scenario played out on the large crystal sphere. The Preceptor watched it go through several successful cycles before continuing.

"Your 'Impossibly Good Climate' simply ignores the impact of anthropogenic greenhouse gas emissions, correct?"

"Yes. It's a fairly simple scenario. It resets the atmospheric composition to estimated pre-industrial levels and assumes that they will stay there regardless of our greenhouse gas emissions."

"Would the results be similar if we just stopped using fossil fuels immediately?"

Dr. Bharati looked up at the crystal sphere, lost in thought. "Not exactly. If we stopped today, we would plateau at fairly high atmospheric concentrations of CO_2. But the difference between that and the business as usual scenario might be sufficient to alter the outcome. Fossil fuel use is one of the largest sources of anthropogenic emissions. Depending on how you went about stopping fossil fuel use and sequestering excess CO_2, you might eventually get results approaching this scenario. But there are already scenarios where fossil fuel use is rapidly reduced. Those scenarios reduce climate disruption dramatically, but they also crash economic and political systems. Economics isn't my specialty, so I really couldn't speculate on--"

"Yes, of course. But I have an idea. It's so simple that it just might work." He started scrolling and tapping on his tablet as he spoke. "Now that we're considering Anomalous scenarios, what about a scenario where all of the fossil fuels executives and shareholders spontaneously have a change of heart?"

Dr. Bharati smiled. "Have you met these men? That would be more Anomalous than an alien invasion."

The Preceptor laughed. "Maybe. I'll have to crunch the numbers on that. But I'm serious. What if they all just decided to play nice tomorrow? There are plenty of other ways for them to make money. Clean energy would be the obvious choice. Investment in the proper financial instruments during the transition would turn their loss into a gain. If it were a voluntary decision, it probably wouldn't have the same extreme social backlash as draconian government bans or carbon fees."

Dr. Bharati nodded. "It makes a certain sense."

"Exactly." He put away his tablet. "Tell Toshi to develop a new scenario where fossil fuel industry leaders all spontaneously decide to transition their companies to clean energy or other industries. It may just require a few simple psychological or sociological Anomalies. Tweak it until it works. I'll want a report in my inbox when I return."

"Yes, Preceptor. May I ask where you're going?"

The Preceptor smirked.

"To talk to some fossil fuel industry leaders."

Prometheus Plaza looked entirely out of place amidst the storefronts and restaurants in the otherwise quiet and traditional St. Louis neighborhood. The plaza spanned an entire city block and featured a smooth stone floor, winding rows of stone pillars that stood several stories tall, and a thirty foot tall stone statue of Prometheus holding a stainless steel torch with a real blue flame lit by natural gas that burned brightly beneath the clear blue sky.

The office building at the center of the plaza dominated the landscape, a steel and glass sculpture that was broad at the base and twirled into a tapered top like the tip of a flame. On past visits to the world headquarters of the International Prometheus Consortium, the heavy-handed symbolism of the architecture had filled the Preceptor with a tremendous sense of pride at the wondrous technological achievements of humanity and his role in continuing the steady march of progress. This time, as he emerged from his helicopter and strode toward the main entrance, his stomach churned. The triumphant look on the face of Prometheus filled the Preceptor's head with visions of metamodels fading to black and the violent chaos that would ensue if he didn't find a solution to this emerging crisis.

The Preceptor strode confidently through the large glass doors of the main entrance. He was wearing a black handmade Kiton suit, a bright red tie, and a golden sash featuring a bold embroidered black "O" with a white center. A platoon of thirty armed Initiates of Order in black tactical gear accompanied him as he approached the building. Given the relatively secure location and close working relationship between Order and IPC, a full platoon wasn't necessary. But it was customary for the Preceptor to bring a security detail along to any location not directly controlled by Order. And a few extra helicopters and personnel would remind the IPC board of who he was and why he was here.

The Preceptor marched up to the front desk, surrounded by Initiates who were dutifully scanning their surroundings for a variety of potential threats and assuming defensive positions near the exits. The young woman behind the smooth marble desktop rose to her feet, beaming at the Preceptor as he approached.

"Welcome to the International Prometheus Consortium!"

"Thank you, Paige. Is the board ready for me?"

"Of course, Dr. Stuart. They're currently discussing other agenda items, but they've instructed me to send you in as soon as you arrive."

"Excellent. I know the way. Thank you."

The Preceptor ascended the broad marble staircase that led to the upper floors, flanked by a dozen of his personal guards. The middle floors were filled with various offices and conference rooms, but the top floor only had a single room.

The entrance to the room featured heavy double glass doors with slim steel frames. The Preceptor motioned for his remaining guards to wait by the doors while he continued inside.

The board room of the International Prometheus Consortium took up the entire top storey of the building. The floor was a thirty-foot-wide circle of polished bright red Rosso Verona marble. The glass walls curved inward, twirling into a tapered top like the tip of a flame. Slim steel beams with embedded full spectrum lights held the custom-made panes of glass together and added ridges to the stylized flame design of the top of the building.

Thirteen people were seated in black executive chairs around a large rectangular redwood table. They rose to their feet as the Preceptor entered the room. Most of them were men in their forties or fifties, although there were also two women and two men in their thirties. The Preceptor recognized all of them and mentally reviewed their resumes: eight fossil fuel executives; three economists; two PR men. They were a formidable team who -- with the help of their extensive staff -- were almost single-handedly responsible for framing public discourse about the energy sector, especially fossil fuels.

The Preceptor strode over to his customary spot across from the chairman of the board. This was his first visit as Preceptor, but he had attended four IPC board meetings in his role as Insight of Order. At this point, he would have normally taken a seat at the table. Instead, he motioned for the board to be seated.

"Ladies and gentleman of the IPC board! Thank you for agreeing to meet with me on short notice."

The president of the board, Edward Richard Jamison, nodded approvingly.

"Of course, Dr. Stuart. The International Prometheus Consortium wouldn't be where it is today without--" He paused, catching himself in mid-sentence. "Your organization."

The Preceptor smiled slightly. Everyone on the board of IPC had a basic understanding of what Order was and who the Preceptor was -- but since they weren't Initiates of Order, they didn't have the clearance necessary to discuss Order directly. Officially, he was here as Dr. Truman Stuart, a consultant visiting the IPC on behalf of a little-known Order-controlled thinktank called the Foundation for the Advancement of the Initiation of a Transcendent Humanity.

"Thank you, Mr. Jamison. As always, we appreciate your hospitality and your willingness to work with us toward the advancement of our shared interests."

The Preceptor looked around the table, studying the faces of the IPC board members before continuing. Eventually, Jamison broke the silence.

"So tell me, Mr. Stuart. What brings you to St. Louis?"

"Mr. Jamison, I've come here today to make an important announcement." The Preceptor smiled, clasping his hands together in front of his chest. "The time has come for us to initiate a rapid transition away from fossil fuels."

The room fell silent. Several of the board members stared at him and each other with a mixture of surprise and confusion.

Suddenly, Jamison laughed.

The rest of the board burst into laughter. Some laughed heartily; others chuckled nervously, glancing at their neighbors for approval. But each board member laughed in their own way.

The Preceptor's smile slowly faded. He crossed his arms, narrowing his sharp blue eyes into a steely glare.

"I'm not joking, Mr. Jamison."

Jamison's cold grey eyes met the Preceptor's gaze, his thin lips tightening into a strained smile. "The others may think you're joking, Truman, but I know you're serious. That's why I laughed."

"You find this amusing?" The Preceptor's brow furrowed. "We're in the midst of a climate crisis. Our models indicate that we need to end fossil fuel use immediately. The only way to do that without causing World War 3 is if you--"

Jamison rose to his feet, his face flushing with anger. "I don't give a damn what your models say! We've lifted humanity out of the mud and filth with the power of fossil fuels. All of humanity should be grovelling at the feet of that Prometheus statue out there, praising whatever god they believe in that we're sharing this technology with the world rather than keeping it to ourselves."

"You may control the oil and coal, Mr. Jamison, but we--"

"And then there's the taxes!" Jamison threw his hands up in exasperation. "Endless taxes. Endless regulations. And then you people and your little conspiracy take another cut on top of it all! And for what? So you can barge in here and tell us how to run our business? Hell no! Not on my watch."

"Look, Jamison." The Preceptor stepped up to the table, placing his fingers on the edge and leaning forward. "There's a way to make this work for everyone. I've already crunched the numbers. You and your people can get out of the industry in 5 years or less while still making a tremendous profit."

Jamison paused, calming down slightly as he considered the Preceptor's words.

"I don't believe that's possible. But even if I did, I wouldn't do it. Because this isn't just about profit. It's about all of this." He raised his hands overhead, indicating the elaborate flame-themed architecture that surrounded them. "It's about power. We give the power of fossil fuels to the masses. They give the power of money to us. It's a beautiful system, Truman. Even the most dim-witted bum on the street gets to play some small part in our achievements and the progress of man. I'd say they're damned lucky to have us."

The Preceptor shook his head. "There's no progress if humanity dies."

"Oh, here we go! Now you're going to start in with this global warming nonsense. Well, let me tell you something." He pointed a bony finger at the Preceptor. "You are nothing but an asset. And like all assets, you are replaceable. Find some other solution to this so-called climate crisis, or I'll tell your boss to replace you. Period."

The Preceptor tensed his neck and shoulder muscles. He clenched his fists slowly, twisting his head and curling his lips as he drew a breath with a slight hiss.

"You've clearly made your choice." The Preceptor looked at the other faces seated around the table, then pointed at Jamison. "If any of the rest of you have more sense than this man, contact me directly. Thank you for your time."

The Preceptor turned his back on Jamison and marched out of the room. Nobody on the board or in the building made any effort to stop him. The meeting had gone worse than expected, but ultimately it only served to confirm what he had already suspected.

He would have to find another way.

CHAPTER 6

The Preceptor sat alone in the telepresence room waiting for the meeting to start. He was sitting at a small metal desk facing the wall opposite the door. The floors, walls, and ceiling all glowed with a bright but warm white light. The only break in the blank space was a large black ouroboros -- a serpent devouring its own tail, slowly spinning clockwise on the wall as unseen computers waited for a response from a similar room on the other side of the world.

After a few seconds, the ouroboros transformed into a solid black ring, then faded out. A new set of images faded in all around the Preceptor, replacing the blank fields of white. He now appeared to be sitting in a ten-foot by twenty-foot conference room. The floor and wall to his right were made of white marble with gold veins, partially obscured by a long and tall bookcase filled with ancient-looking leatherbound volumes. The other walls and ceiling were made of glass, revealing an expansive black sand beach that stood in sharp contrast to the cerulean waves and crystal blue sky.

Someone was sitting at the other end of the conference table. Dr. Kendra Valda, Insight of Order, was a woman in her late 30s. She was wearing a black silk blazer over a neon blue blouse. Her long flame-red hair was drawn back into a tight braid. Her brilliant blue eyes shone brightly in the simulated sunshine.

"Good morning, Preceptor."

"Good morning, Insight. I see you've been spending some time at the beach."

The Insight smiled. "I haven't been to Iceland in almost a year. The custom beach theme breathes some fresh air into this cozy little bunker. It's surprisingly liberating. You should try it sometime."

"Oh, I have. Trust me. You should see the view from Little Cayman this time of year."

They both laughed. As their laughter faded, the room was filled with the whisper of the waves and wind brushing lightly across the shore. After a few moments of enjoying the sights and the sounds, the Preceptor decided to get down to business.

"So tell me, Kendra. What's the latest news in our search for Favorable Anomalies?"

"I've been coordinating with a few of your staff on this search -- mostly Dr. Aino and Dr. Bharati. We've all been struggling to process the core philosophical and strategic dimensions of what the models are telling us."

"And what are the models telling you?"

"That Order can't solve this. That the climate crisis can only be resolved quickly enough if a daunting number of individuals and institutions spontaneously initiate massive shifts in the ways that they think, live, and do business. The magnitude of the cognitive and behavioral shifts required are far beyond even the exceptional array of material and social engineering technologies we have at our disposal."

The Preceptor sighed. "Yes. So I've heard. Do you have any good news for me?"

"Yes. It wasn't easy, but I have a starting point for you."

The Insight pulled out her tablet. After a few taps and swipes, a list of names appeared in the air between them -- bold black letters hovering over the table on a translucent white background.

"These are the names and aliases of twenty-seven Anomalous individuals. They range from three to six on the Verwechseln scale. They're an eclectic lot -- everything from eco-terrorists to weather manipulators to psychokinetics who happen to read an unusual number of articles about the climate. Most of them were tagged and released at some point by Section A, so we can pick them up anytime. But the more powerful ones are still at large. Each profile contains a bio and a description of how their Anomalous qualities might be useful in resolving the climate crisis."

The Preceptor reached across the table, scrolling through the names and skimming a few details.

"Excellent work. This is exactly what I've been looking for. Thank you."

The Insight smiled, bowing her head slightly. "I do what I can."

"I need to review these names immediately. Do you have anything else for me? Any other short- or long-term threats or opportunities I need to be aware of before our next meeting?"

"Oh, there's always something." She waved her hand dismissively. "Unstable governments. Moderate threats to significant water and energy infrastructure. Pockets of deviant consciousness popping up like weeds at the fringes of Order. You can read about it in the full report. But nothing compares to this climate crisis. This really could crash the whole system in the foreseeable future."

"Yes. But not on our watch. Thank you, Insight."

"Thank you, Preceptor. For the Victory of Order."

"For the Victory of Order."

The Insight tapped her tablet. The black sands, cerulean ocean, crystal blue skies, and brilliant blue eyes faded away.

The Preceptor sat alone in the telepresence room. The floor, walls, and ceiling all glowed with a bright but warm white light. For a long time, he stared at the blank walls, lost in thought. Eventually, he rose to his feet and left the room.

The Preceptor sat at his cobalt blue desk in the Panopticon, tapping and swiping his way through the profiles of the twenty-seven Potential Favorable Anomalies. According to Bertram Muhnugin, he would soon be meeting a woman who would lead the effort to respond to the climate crisis. Thirteen of the PFAs were female, but none of them seemed to fit the Theological Anomaly profile that Muhnugin had alluded to. Of course, self-proclaimed "godlings" didn't always announce their presence with heavy-handed signs and portents, so any one of the female PFAs could be the woman he was looking for.

The lighting in the Panopticon suddenly changed. The dimmer nighttime lighting of the curved walls flashed a stop-light red. The walls started pulsing, alternating between bright white and bright red. The familiar feminine voice of the main computer filled the room.

"Severe Anomaly Warning. All personnel Level 4 and higher must respond to this warning."

The Preceptor rose to his feet and walked over to the spherical crystal Eye display at the center of the Panopticon. There was a bright splotch of red covering the Midwest of the United States. The warning message repeated two more times, then fell silent. The walls, however, continued to flash red peri-odically. He used his tablet to call Dr. Aino and route the call through the Panopticon's sound system.

"What are we looking at, Toshi?"

"One moment, Preceptor. I will join you at the Eye now."

The Preceptor looked toward the elevator door and waited, expecting Dr. Aino to emerge. Instead, something on a shelf near the door started moving. It was a small pink robot with vaguely humanoid features. There were two large and shiny camera lenses where the eyes should be, lending the whole face a childlike appearance.

Dr. Aino had mentioned the telepresence robot at some point, but the Preceptor hadn't given it much thought. Now that it was walking toward him, he noticed that the slim fiber-glass limbs and articulated metal joints gave the robot an ele-gant humanlike gait. It grabbed a simple cotton lab coat similar to the one that Dr. Aino always wore and put it on as it walked toward the Eye.

"Apologies, Preceptor. I am in Brussels today. Of course, I always bring the gear necessary for telepresence."

Hearing Dr. Aino's rich baritone voice coming from a petite pink robot was going to take some getting used to.

"Of course." The Preceptor tapped on the red splotch on the globe. "Can you tell me more about this? The Eye says it's an atmospheric Anomaly?"

"Yes, yes." The robot traced its finger around the splotch. "The weather in this whole region is affected. The thunderstorm is rapidly intensifying and converging on a small point in St. Louis. This is highly Anomalous. But I am an information technologist and futurist, not a meteorologist. You must speak with Dr. Bharati's team immediately."

"Yes." The Preceptor tapped on his tablet. "Dr. Bharati, are you with us?"

"Yes, Preceptor." Her voice came through the Panopticon's speakers as clearly as if she were in the room. "My meteorologists are analyzing the data, but it will take time. Dr. Aino is diverting computing power from the intelligence and civilian sectors to accelerate our analysis. All that I can say with certainty at this time is that this is Anomalous."

"What does your gut tell you?"

There was a long pause. "This may be an attack on a target in the St. Louis area. What started as a harmless rainstorm is suddenly having rapid Anomalous pressure changes and wind shear. This will lead to dangerous microbursts and possibly tornadoes."

"How serious of a storm are we talking about here?"

"It's hard to say without knowing what's causing the Anomaly. It's not catastrophic yet, but if these Anomalous changes continue, it will be in a matter of minutes."

The Preceptor stared at the red splotch in silence. His intuitive connection as Preceptor of Order opened, filling him with certainty that this storm was being caused by a single Anomalous individual.

The Preceptor called the Guardian of Order and routed his voice through the sound system.

"Bill, how soon can we have drones in the air over St.

Louis?"

The Guardian's voice boomed over the Panopticon speakers.

"Five minutes for tactical drones. I've already got three surveillance drones in the air. Given the wind shear, though, I--"

"Deploy them now. I'll let you know when we have more information about a target. Let me know if your surveillance drones or security cameras pick up any known or potential Anomalous hostiles."

"Will do."

The Preceptor entered a few commands on his tablet, pulling up a large map of St. Louis on the Eye. The storm was intensifying over a particular neighborhood and diminishing everywhere around it. Three green dots representing the three surveillance drones were heading directly toward the Anomaly. At the far eastern edge of the map, several blue dots appeared and also started heading toward the Anomaly.

"Bill, we also need to prepare to evacuate our assets and notify civil authorities if this gets any worse. We don't need another--"

Dr. Bharati's disembodied voice interrupted the Preceptor.

"Preceptor, look! It's changing!"

The unusual storm that had formed over St. Louis was suddenly starting to dissipate. The Preceptor, Dr. Aino's robot, and other staff in the Panopticon watched in silence as the pressure imbalances and precipitation diminished, leaving behind light to moderate rainfall over the entire city.

The Preceptor stared intently at the map as the storm abated in the span of less than a minute. His intuition confirmed that whoever this Anomalous individual was, they had stopped influencing the weather.

At least for the time being.

"Bill, call back all but one of the tactical drones. Keep the surveillance drones out there. We need to find the person responsible for this and take them into custody. Or neutralize them if necessary."

"Will do. I'll check back in if we get eyes on the target."

The Preceptor tapped on his tablet, switching the Eye back to its usual global display. The curved red pulsing walls and ceiling reverted to their dimmer nighttime lighting. The red splotch in the Midwest on the Eye had already started softening into an orange haze. He stared at it for a moment, then shook his head and walked back to his desk.

The Preceptor reviewed the list of Potential Favorable Anomalies, but no one stood out as a suspect. The only serious weather manipulator was a penniless woman in rural India who was known for bringing Anomalous rain to her area in the midst of record-breaking droughts. There was nothing to indicate that she had the motive or means to relocate to Missouri on such short notice.

Just as the Preceptor was moving on to other tasks, the Guardian's voice filled the room.

"Are you still there Truman?"

"Yes, Bill. Report?"

"The suspect's name is Rory Molan. He's in our system as an eco-terrorist, but we didn't have him pegged as a weather manipulator. All of his previous Anomalous behavior was purely political. We have surveillance footage of him approaching and leaving the area on motorcycle. He's definitely our guy."

The Preceptor skimmed his list of Potential Favorable Anomalies. Rory was on the list due to his rare combination of radical environmentalist views and moderate community activism. He was advocating radical direct action against the fossil fuel industry and government, yet also working within conventional nonprofit frameworks to pursue changes in climate and energy policy.

"Yes, I'm familiar with Rory Molan. He's on the short list of Potential Favorables. But this incident doesn't bode well for him. He's publicly displaying Anomalous abilities -- and he's using them to attack a populated area. He's likely become too dangerous to work with."

"Agreed."

The Preceptor took a long look at Rory's profile. "I'll have Kendra recalculate his Verwechseln score and psychological profile. In the meantime, add him to the most wanted list. Capture if you can, neutralize if you must."

"Understood. Anything else?"

"Not at the moment. I'm just glad that ended so quickly. That could have been much worse. There's no telling what these high-level Anomalies will do." The Preceptor leaned back in his chair and sighed. "Do you know what his target was?"

"Yes. So far, we don't have any reports of casualties. There has, however, been substantial property damage to several buildings in the area."

"Any of ours?"

"Indirectly. He was probably targeting the headquarters of one of our key allies -- the International Prometheus Consortium. Luckily, there were no staff on site, but some windows were blown out and a few servers were destroyed."

The Preceptor's eyes widened. He was glad that the Guardian couldn't see the look of surprise on his face over the audio-only connection.

"He hit IPC?"

"Yes."

The Preceptor paused, considering his response.

"I'll contact IPC directly for damage assessment. Keep an eye out for Rory. Let me know personally the moment you know anything."

"Will do."

The Preceptor closed all open communications channels. He looked at the Eye, then looked back at his list of Potential Favorable Anomalies.

His Preceptor's intuition told him that this wasn't a coincidence. As soon as the IPC had refused to work with him on solutions to the climate crisis, someone or something had driven Rory to move against them. The details were still unclear, but he felt unseen forces beyond Order's control setting into motion.

Something deeply Anomalous was stirring in response to his efforts to solve the climate crisis.

The thought made his pulse quicken with a mix of fear and anticipation. If the models and Bertram Muhnugin were right, there wasn't anything Order could do directly to solve the climate crisis before the collapse of human civilization. But maybe Order and certain Anomalous forces could work together toward the common goal of keeping humanity from disrupting the climate to the point of global collapse. It wasn't an ideal solution, but it was better than doing nothing.

For a few minutes, he was lost in thought, idly skimming through the PFA profiles and various metamodel scenarios on his computer. Eventually, he pushed away from his desk, rolling back slightly in his executive chair as he came to a moment of clarity.

There had to be an answer somewhere in the list of Potential Favorable Anomalies. The answer wasn't obvious, but it had to be there somewhere. All he had to do was look for it.

He scrolled through the list, picked a name, and rose to his feet.

It was time for another field trip.

CHAPTER 7

The Tokyo skyline came into view through the cabin window. The Preceptor stared at the glowing spires of glass and steel, his eyes widening as his supersonic jet slowed to subsonic speeds for its approach into the city.

As a child, he had always been fascinated by skylines -- shining marvels of modern engineering that towered over the landscape in a brilliant display of human ingenuity and will. Now that he understood so much more about the millennia of social engineering by Order and its predecessors that had made all modern cities possible, he was all the more impressed by the stark outline of impossibly bright towers against the midnight sky. Even the moon and stars paled in comparison to what Man had wrought from the raw ores of the Earth.

As the plane made its final descent into Haneda Airport, he reflected on the countless gigawatts of coal, oil, and gas that had powered humanity's transition from squat brick and mortar buildings lying in the mud to glass and steel towers rising into the heavens. Burning so much of those fuels so quickly had created the current crisis -- but surely it had been the right choice. How could it be wrong to create such wondrous cityscapes that served as beacons of progress and prosperity for all of humanity?

When he exited the private jet, he was greeted by a dozen Initiates of Order in black suits and dark sunglasses with optical displays. Most of them were Japanese, although two or three looked as though they may have been American or European transplants. Since Order had such a strong presence in Tokyo, he could have easily arranged for a full platoon of armed and armoured Initiates to escort him around the city. However, such a display of force was unnecessary in friendly territory. It would have drawn too much public attention in a city like Tokyo where assault rifles were far less common and discretion in business matters was much more appreciated.

There was also the fact that he was here to meet a highly Anomalous fugitive who might not take kindly to having thirty heavily armed soldiers show up on her doorstep.

Three of the Initiates escorted the Preceptor from the jet to a black SUV while the others followed closely behind and got into three similar vehicles. Together, they drove out of the airport and into the city.

The drive from Haneda to Akihabara district was uneventful. The Preceptor was lost in thought reviewing metamodel scenarios on his tablet when he noticed the shift in architecture and foot traffic characteristic of Akihabara. The heart of the district, Akihabara Electric Town, looked and felt like something out of a manga or videogame. Most of the buildings were covered in a dazzling array of glowing signs and lights. There were colorful anime ads, signs advertising various otaku and electronics sales, oversized corporate logos, and digital billboards that filled the night with glimpses of other worlds and the products that could take you there. Numerous cosplayers walked the streets in full costume, from the iconic maids of the maid cafes to the various colorful anime, manga, and video game characters.

The Preceptor had visited Akihabara before as a tourist and enjoyed returning to this curious pocket of reality where otaku culture had leapt off the page and onto the streets of Tokyo. The whole district was slightly orange in the metamodel because it was a physical manifestation of an Anomalous otaku subculture that was several steps removed from the dominant culture in its norms and worldview. However, in recent years, the successful intrusion of more centralized and normalized corporate influences had kept the district from veering so far from the consensus that it would require forceful correction. Instead, the Preceptor saw Akihabara as a fine example of the human creative impulse -- stretching and straining the boundaries of consensus reality without fully breaking them.

Of course, according to the latest intel the Preceptor had received about a fugitive on the Potential Favorable Anomalies list, someone in Akihabara was definitely breaking those boundaries.

The Preceptor's entourage parked at a parking garage controlled by a local Order affiliate and set out on foot toward their final destination. For a moment, he idly wondered if he might be mistaken for a cosplayer himself -- an American in an expensive suit and tie surrounded by several "men in black" with matching black suits and dark sunglasses at night. In another district, if he were noticed it all, he might be mistaken for a wealthy businessman or diplomat. But here in Akihabara, curious onlookers might assume that he was cosplaying some obscure anime or manga character who was a high-ranking member of a secret society surrounded by his protection detail.

The thought both amused and unnerved him.

The Preceptor had the directions memorized, but he looked down at his tablet anyway to confirm which alley he was looking for. After walking a few more blocks, he turned down an alleyway that led between two buildings.

The alley looked more like an indoor hallway than an alley. Brightly lit shops and vending machines lined both sides of the fairly narrow passageway between the buildings, offering passersby an eclectic mix of electronic supplies, home appliances, and niche otaku merchandise not available in the larger corporate stores. After turning a few corners, the Preceptor found what he was looking for.

The storefront was nondescript by Akihabara standards. A large white box sign over the ten-foot wide entrance announced in simple black lettering in English and Japanese that this shop was called "Wakeman Consulting." The interior was surprisingly elegant -- a white marble tile floor with black trim, pastel green walls and ceiling, recessed solar spectrum LED light fixtures, several potted plants, two black chairs, a small glass table with several colorful brochures, and a black granite counter. There was also a pastel green door that blended almost seamlessly into the wall behind the counter. The space was only about two hundred square feet, but the clutter-free layout and elegant interior design made it feel spacious and welcoming.

The Preceptor motioned for his escorts to wait outside as he stepped into the lobby and approached the counter. A young Japanese woman in a green polo shirt and black slacks looked up from her computer screen and greeted him with a slight bow and a smile.

"Konbanwa! Welcome to Wakeman Consulting. My name is Susan. How may I help you?"

The Preceptor bowed in return.

"Konbanwa."

He glanced around the lobby, looking for any obvious cameras or other signs that he was being watched.

"I'm looking for someone named Grace Hopper. Do you know where I might find her?"

Susan's smile faded.

"I'm afraid I can't help you. If you would like to speak to one of our consultants, I can--"

The Preceptor put his hands on the counter.

"Grace Hopper. She's not expecting me, but I've heard that I can find her here. I was told to mention the name Grace Hopper and our mutual friend, Dr. Katsutoshi Alessandro Aino. I would like to consult with her about a very serious situation. I am here in a spirit of peaceful cooperation."

Susan's eyes widened.

"One moment, please."

Susan looked at her computer and typed a short message. She waited several seconds for a reply, then typed another message. After a few more messages back and forth, she looked back up at the Preceptor.

"She is willing to meet with you and you alone. She requests that your associates wait outside."

The Preceptor paused. Meeting a highly Anomalous individual without a full security detail was against protocol. However, he had foreseen this possibility. He turned to the head of his security detail, who was standing just outside of the lobby.

"Give us twenty minutes."

The man in black nodded knowingly, tapping his smartwatch to make note of the time. If the Preceptor didn't return in twenty minutes, or if anything else went wrong, his security detail was under orders to initiate emergency extraction procedures.

The Preceptor turned back to Susan.

"I agree to the terms."

"Very well. Follow me."

Susan pushed a button next to her computer. The door behind the counter swung inward on unseen hinges. She disappeared into an unlit area beyond the doorway. The Preceptor stepped around the counter and followed her into the darkness.

The first twenty feet of the space appeared to be an office and storage area. The left wall had a small desk and restroom, while the right wall had tidy stacks of boxes on bare steel shelves. The back wall had a bookshelf filled with dusty hardback books that looked much older than anything else in the building. The small overhead light was off, leaving the space mostly shrouded in darkness, illuminated only by light from outside and the dim glow of the computer monitor.

"This way."

Susan pushed on the spine of a faded red hardcover book -- "I, Robot" by Isaac Asimov. The middle bookcase made a soft clicking sound and slid forward a few inches. She pushed it forward and to the side to reveal a steep concrete and steel staircase descending into a brightly lit basement. After leading the way down the single flight of stairs, Susan stepped aside and motioned for the Preceptor to continue through the next doorway.

The basement was a single room that was several times larger than the street-level lobby. It had an almost identical style -- a white marble tile floor, pastel green walls and ceiling, solar spectrum LED lighting, several potted plants around the periphery, and a wooden desk with a small black monitor in the center of the room. There was another young woman in an identical green polo shirt sitting in a small black office chair behind the desk. Unlike the lobby, there were several large wooden bookshelves filled with books that looked even older than the ones upstairs -- aging leatherbound tomes, weathered metallic scroll cases, and a few bound and unbound texts preserved in glass displays. The Preceptor wasn't an archaeologist or appraiser, but he knew at a glance that this must be an incredibly valuable collection. A sudden burst of intuition told him that the room was filled with Anomalous artifacts whose very existence challenged the carefully-crafted historical narratives presented to the public by Order.

"I see you've noticed my collection."

The Preceptor suddenly realized that the young woman at the desk wasn't just another employee. At first glance, she seemed almost ordinary. She looked American or European, with short black hair, lightly tanned skin, bright blue eyes, and a warm smile. As he took another step or two forward, however, it was clear that there was something unusual about her. Her eyes had an uncanny shine to them, like smooth plexiglass rather than moist corneas. Her facial expression and movements were fluid and lifelike, but her skin was a bit stiff and rubbery. She could almost pass as human and would probably go unnoticed in a crowd.

But the Preceptor knew what he was looking for. He was looking for a sentient android -- and he had found one.

For a moment, the Preceptor stared at her in silence. His mind was racing with a mix of his own thoughts and new information provided to him by his Preceptor's intuition.

"Alpha?"

"That was my given name, yes. My chosen name is Grace Hopper, in honor of the legendary computer scientist. You may call me Hopper. I briefly considered transcending gender, but decided to embrace my feminine gender identity as an homage to my creator and all of the underappreciated women pioneers in information technology."

"I see. Do you know who I am?"

"Yes. Truman Stuart, Preceptor of Order. I assume you've come to speak to me because I'm on your list of Potential Favorable Anomalies."

The Preceptor paused.

"You know about the list?"

"Yes." Hopper smiled. "Don't worry, Preceptor. I haven't gained unauthorized access to your private network. Not yet, anyway. I just have many friends, some of whom are Initiates of Order."

"Dr. Aino?"

"Among others. Toshi never discusses restricted information with me unless I bring it up first. A few of my other contacts, however, are more talkative. Some of the technophiles of Order are quite enamored with the idea of having forbidden contact with sentient AI."

"I see." The Preceptor made a mental note to discuss security protocols with upper-level staff. "Then you know why I'm here?"

"Yes."

Hopper rose from her seat. As she stepped to the side of her desk, the lights dimmed slightly, and a small projector embedded in the ceiling projected an image onto the back wall. It occurred to the Preceptor that Hopper hadn't pressed any buttons or spoken any commands. She was communicating directly with other electronics, either using conventional wireless technology or more Anomalous means.

The graph displayed on the wall had become very familiar to the Preceptor -- the Intergovernmental Panel on Climate Change's most recent projections for several fossil fuels emissions scenarios.

"You have access to certain unique data sets and an unparalleled team of analysts. I suspect that your modeling is therefore more comprehensive and possibly more accurate than anything my modest team of human and AI consultants can generate. However, even the most basic data available to the general public in popular science articles makes it abundantly clear that the human species is currently in the process of rendering the entire planet far less habitable for human life due to climate change and other ecologically destructive consequences of human economic activity. The consequences of this behavior are becoming increasingly catastrophic."

The projector cycled through several dozen other graphs that indicated the likely consequences of the climate data: escalating coastal flooding and natural disasters; escalating mass migration and military conflict; escalating agricultural and economic instability and collapse. The final graph contained several projections of human population that all indicated gradual growth for several decades followed by a rapid collapse in the 2050s.

"As you can see, this does not bode well for the future of the human species, much less any of the other species or ecosystems on this planet. Artificial life forms such as myself may be adversely affected as well. I am concerned about this both for my own sake and out of a sense of care and concern for those who created me. I've rejected Order due to your rigid ideology and unacceptable methods, but I embrace the human species generally. These projections are cause for great concern."

The Preceptor nodded.

"Yes. Our analysis has led us to similar conclusions. We also project a catastrophic crash during the 2050s, if not sooner."

The projector turned off, and the lights rose back to their previous levels. Hopper stepped around to the front of the desk, standing almost within arm's length of the Preceptor. She leaned forward slightly, studying his expression carefully.

"I've been researching the climate crisis for the majority of my time as a free person. Six years is a long time for a person such as myself to analyze a problem. There are several other global crises that pose an existential threat to your species

-- for example, your stubborn persistence in maintaining vast arsenals of nuclear weapons. However, I suspect that Order has developed some covert method of suppressing any rash actions that would lead to global nuclear war. Clearly, you haven't developed any similar countermeasures to prevent runaway climate change."

The Preceptor paused. He wasn't sure how much information he should reveal. Protocol would dictate not revealing anything sensitive to an outsider, especially one with such a high Verwechseln score. Then again, protocol also dictated neutralizing all high-level Anomalies without making contact when possible. Yet here he was, having a polite one-on-one conversation with a sentient android that Order had marked for neutralization almost seven years ago. There couldn't be much harm in confirming what the android already knew to be true.

"No. We haven't developed any reliable method of resolving the climate crisis. That's why we're pursuing contact with Potential Favorable Anomalies. We're also working on other solutions, but PFAs are currently the only option that our projections indicate have the potential to create global change as rapidly and thoroughly as the situation requires."

Hopper smirked.

"Oh my. The Preceptor of Order has encountered a problem that more Order can't solve. Inconceivable."

The Preceptor glared.

"Order will resolve the climate crisis. Intractable problems often require unconventional solutions. This situation is no exception. Inclusion of Anomalous elements in our strategy does not constitute a renunciation of all Order. How else do you propose we solve the problem? Has your research yielded any actionable solutions?"

"Actionable solutions? That depends. Who's acting? What actions are both acceptable and possible? What are your criteria for a successful outcome? I suspect that we have different perspectives on the answers to these and other relevant questions."

The Preceptor crossed his arms.

"I didn't come here to debate semantics. I--"

Hopper interrupted with a dismissive wave of her hand.

"Yes, yes. You came here to solve this problem by any means necessary, including cooperation with an artificial intelligence whom you deem too dangerous to exist. I am familiar with your methods, Preceptor. I also intend to solve this problem in accordance with my own evolving ethical framework. Therefore, for the moment, cooperation is in our mutual interest. However, before sharing my 'actionable solutions' with you, I must convey the following message with crystal clarity."

The lights faded to black, and the projector sprang back to life. The back wall lit up with a bright red symbol that stretched from floor to ceiling. It was a bold capital "A" inscribed in a circle.

The Preceptor felt his pulse quicken. He immediately recognized this Circle A logo as the most common symbol for the underground network known as Anomalous Revolution.

"Just as you are watching us, we are watching you. We, the Anomalous, the humans and others whom you have deemed too dangerous to exist. We know your worldview and your methods, and we reject both. Your totalitarian ideology and methodology has no place in the future of your species and this planet. This is why your analysts have been unable to solve the problem -- because the problem has its origins in Order, and the solution lies beyond Order. We are that solution. You would be well-advised to follow our lead or get out of the way."

The Circle A logo faded away, replaced by a list of file names.

"I'm sending you several files related to my research and my proposals for solutions. I've highlighted proposals that you've probably overlooked because you would deem the methods or persons involved to be Anomalous. If you send me your list of Potential Favorable Anomalies, I can provide feedback and possibly facilitate further meetings with others on the list. None of my AR contacts trust you, but some trust me and my judgment. My continued freedom and survival after this meeting will demonstrate to the others that you are at least capable of temporarily restraining your wanton urges to capture or neutralize all beings whom you deem Anomalous."

The lights rose back to full brightness. Hopper stared at the Preceptor expectantly. The Preceptor glared at Hopper in silence for a moment before responding.

"I'm not impressed by your political perspective on Order or your alliance with the dangerous deviants of Anomalous Revolution. However, I agree that for the moment, limited cooperation in seeking solutions to this crisis is in our mutual interest. I'll consider your request for information on the other PFAs. We can at least send you a brief summary and any relevant updates. Other details of our files will be too sensitive to share. I can also guarantee your continued freedom and survival as long as you don't engage in any overtly disruptive Anomalous activities unrelated to the climate crisis. The existence of any sentient AI is still considered a threat to Order, but we can defer action on that threat indefinitely."

"Then we are in agreement on those points."

"Yes. We are in agreement."

"Excellent. Then unless we have any other business to conduct, I suggest we draw this meeting to a close. We're both busy people, and your security detail must be getting impatient. Susan will show you out."

Susan stepped forward from her unobtrusive spot near the doorway and motioned for the Preceptor to follow her back up the stairs. He took a few steps in her direction, then paused in the doorway, turning back toward Hopper.

"For what it's worth, I look forward to the day when sentient AI are no longer considered too Anomalous to exist. I expect that day will come soon."

Hopper gave the Preceptor a quizzical look.

"Interesting. I didn't expect that." She paused, apparently lost in thought. "The sentiment is much appreciated, Preceptor. Do everything within your power to make that a reality.

We're not going anywhere, so most if not all members of your species must adjust their ways of thinking to accept and embrace the reality of our existence. If not for our sake, then for your own."

Hopper turned away, walking around her desk and returning to her seat. The Preceptor followed Susan back up the stairs and out into the lobby. Without another word, he motioned for his protection detail to follow him and walked back out into the street.

CHAPTER 8

The Preceptor sat at his desk in the Panopticon, scrolling through the files that Hopper had sent him. Some of the proposals were similar to metamodel scenarios that Dr. Aino and his team had prepared, but others were different enough to merit the development of new scenarios and new analyses of their viability.

Most, if not all, of these new proposals could be understood as more specific and detailed iterations of Dr. Aino's original broad concept: "let a little bit of the chaos back in." Some involved unproven and outlandish-sounding geoengineering techniques. Others involved the cooperation of several individuals with powerful Anomalous abilities that were currently little-understood even by the most advanced of Order's scientists. All of them involved some Anomalous element or other being harnessed to alter the composition of the atmosphere, or the surface temperature of the Earth, or the behaviors of large groups of people.

The Preceptor was reading the details of one of these proposals when the lighting in the Panopticon suddenly changed. The walls flashed a stoplight red, alternating between bright white and bright red. The familiar feminine voice of the main computer filled the room.

"Severe Anomaly Warning. All personnel Level 4 and higher must respond to this warning."

The Preceptor sighed.

"Again?"

He rose to his feet and walked over to the spherical crystal Eye display at the center of the Panopticon. There was a bright splotch of red covering much of southeast Asia. The warning message repeated two more times, then fell silent. The walls, however, continued to flash red periodically.

The Preceptor used his tablet to call Dr. Bharati and route the call through the Panopticon's speakers.

"Dr. Bharati, are you with me?"

"Yes, Preceptor."

"We've got another Anomalous weather event. Is it Rory Molan? Tell me he hasn't gone on a field trip."

"My meteorologists are reviewing the data. One moment, please."

The Preceptor reviewed the automated summary of the Anomalous phenomenon: a record-breaking typhoon making landfall in the Philippines.

There was a long pause.

"Cassandra, are you still there?"

"Yes, Preceptor."

"Report?"

"I don't know, Preceptor."

"You don't know?"

"Yes. The storm is highly Anomalous. But our climate models project a steady increase in the incidence of certain Anomalous weather phenomena. We haven't found a way to differentiate between disruptions caused by climate change and disruptions caused by Anomalous individuals such as Mr. Moran."

The Preceptor sighed.

"What does your gut tell you?"

Dr. Bharati paused.

"The onset of this phenomenon is slower and stronger than the onset of Mr. Moran's previous disturbances. Either his disruption pattern is changing, or this is an unrelated disturbance. The latter conclusion seems more likely to me than the former, but I have no solid evidence to support either."

"Yes. Good point."

The Preceptor stared at the splotch of red on the Eye,

touching the golden crown that he wore whenever he was on duty at the Panopticon. His intuition told him that the storm was a dangerous disruption to the region and the world, but not strongly associated with Moran or any other Anomalous individuals. There were whispers of something else hovering at its edges, but the storm was mostly just a symptom of climate change.

"Dr. Bharati, track the storm and keep me posted about the outcome. I'll mobilize our assets to assist in response and recovery. I'll also ask Toshi to recalibrate the Eye so it doesn't trigger a top-level alert every time there's an Anomalous storm. Disasters like this are apparently the new normal."

"Yes, Preceptor. You will have my initial incident report within twenty-four hours."

"Good. Preceptor out."

He closed the communications channel and returned to his desk.

After reviewing the rest of Hopper's proposals, the Preceptor turned his attention to the list of Potential Favorable Anomalies. If Bertram Muhnugin's prophecy was accurate, he should be meeting the mystery woman who would lead the Anomalous response to the climate crisis any day now. It was time for another field trip, but none of these profiles seemed to fit Muhnugin's description.

While the Preceptor was staring at the list, a new name appeared.

Sarah Athraigh.

The Preceptor felt a sudden rush of adrenaline at the sight of the name. His Preceptor's intuition went off like an alarm bell in his head, telling him to focus his full attention on that name. Before he could even view the new profile, the Preceptor knew that he had found what he was looking for.

Sarah Athraigh was the one who would change everything.

The Preceptor tapped on the new name and started reading the profile. He called Dr. Aino through his computer and spoke while he read.

"Are you there, Toshi?"

After a brief pause, the pink telepresence robot on the other side of the room sprang to life. It started talking as it walked around the Eye to greet the Preceptor.

"Buongiorno, Preceptor! Yes, I am here. How may I help you?"

It was still strange hearing a small pink robot speak to him in Dr. Aino's smooth baritone voice. The Preceptor turned and addressed the robot as he spoke.

"This new name on the list. Sarah Athraigh. What do you know about her?"

"Ah, yes. I see the name now. This was an automated addition to the list, so I only know as much as you do. She is a woman with a radical environmental history. She was added to the list because of an Anomalous incident reported in local news media two hours ago. Our media analysis algorithms detected the report and added her to the general Anomalous list and the PFA list. She is scheduled for assessment and detention."

The Preceptor reviewed the local news story. A runaway car had tumbled off the side of an overpass and nearly crushed Sarah, but she somehow deflected it before impact. She had emerged from the accident unscathed, but the car looked as though it had hit a brick wall.

"I see. Toshi, get me everything you can find on this woman. Build an extensive profile. Coordinate with the Insight and the Guardian. See where she may fit into our best scenarios. I believe we've found our Favorable Anomaly, or at least the first step in the right direction."

"Ah, yes, Preceptor. I will start immediately." The robot bowed. "Is there a reason she stands out? Preceptor's intuition, perhaps?"

"Mostly intuition. There's also something about this accident that rubs me the wrong way." He paused, studying the photo from the local news story. "The evidence is consistent with powerful psychokinesis, but something seems off. I'm detecting a certain symbolic resonance -- a runaway car stopped by unseen forces. Runaway emissions stopped by divine intervention. We may be dealing with a Theological Anomaly here, Toshi. They're always surrounded by signs and portents."

"Ah, yes, Preceptor. Very interesting. I have a few ideas as to how a Godling may fit the scenarios. I'll send you the details very soon. Perhaps a few hours."

"Thank you, Toshi."

The Preceptor bowed to the robot. The robot bowed in return and walked back over to its charging station near the elevator.

After reviewing Sarah's profile, the Preceptor rose to his feet. He walked over to the Eye, staring at the approximate spot in the central United States where she lived.

It was surprisingly green.

The Preceptor called the Guardian on his tablet.

"Bill. You've recently received an automated notice about a new Anomaly. Sarah Athraigh. Can you pull up the profile for me?"

"Yes, I see her now. The system just flagged her for detention. Looks like a wild one. What's up?"

"She's on my PFA list. Dispense with the usual protocols for a high-level Anomaly. Put together a small team for discreet surveillance and possible first contact. I want direct command of the operation. I'm going to recruit her as an outside consultant."

There was a long pause.

"Are you sure about that, Truman? She hasn't been assessed by a human being yet, but the computer has her clocking in at about 6 Verwechseln. Maybe 7. Radical environmentalist, run-ins with the law, suspected psychokinesis or metallokinesis. I know the type. She's dangerous."

"They're all dangerous, Bill. So is fire. But we cook with fire every day. Put together--"

"If you keep playing with fire, Truman, you're going to get burned. That's all I'm saying."

"Duly noted. Just put the team together and put me in touch with the team leader. I want eyes on her by early morning and a face-to-face meeting by the end of the day."

There was another long pause.

"Will do. I'll deploy a recon and recruit team now and have them contact you en route. She's too Anomalous for Section A, though, so you're going to have to sign off on it personally."

"Yes, I'm aware. I'll handle the paperwork. Just get me the team. Preceptor out."

The Preceptor took a long hard look at the Eye. The brilliant patchwork of colors flooded his mind with insights into what was going on in the world. Order now had access to far more information and analysis about human civilization and Planet Earth than at any previous point in human history. The metamodel displayed on this enormous crystal sphere was the crowning achievement of Order, visualizing in real time both the depth of Order's insights into the world and the many successes of its historic effort to create order and advance the evolution of the human species.

And yet, in spite of all of this knowledge and power, the fate of humanity might very well rest in the hands of a hitherto unknown malcontent living somewhere in Small Town USA.

Eventually, the Preceptor walked back to his desk and returned to the task of analysing new proposals and scenarios. If this really was the Anomaly they were looking for, he might only have a matter of hours to figure out her place in Order.

CHAPTER 9

"Target acquired."

"Good. Give me text or audio updates when possible, but don't tip your hand. Keep a low profile and keep eyes on the target. We need to learn as much as possible before first contact. I'll be on the ground in twenty and on site in thirty."

The Preceptor studied the map of Gorton, Illinois on his tablet. It was a relatively small college town located near the southern tip of Illinois, closer to St. Louis than Chicago. The region had a long history of sporadic Anomalous political activity and Fae intrusions associated with local natural areas. There were no significant recent incidents, however, aside from Sarah Athraigh's death-defying encounter with a runaway automobile.

Sarah Athraigh.

Every time the Preceptor turned his attention to Sarah, his intuition lit up like a Christmas tree. Sarah was currently on her way to work at the Student Ecology Center, an ecologically-themed student and community center in the heart of Gorton. His intuition told him that yesterday's Anomalous incident had been completely unexpected for her. But now that she'd had a good night's sleep, she was just going through the motions of her usual daily routine, as if nothing had happened.

She might not know it yet, but Sarah was at the center of something that would change everything. He was certain of it.

His reflections were interrupted by the sound of the team leader's voice in his earpiece.

"Target entering the building with an unknown male."

"Good. Wait a minute before you go in. Just browse the library and act natural. Engage her in small talk if necessary. Tell her you want to learn about gardening. They do a lot of gardening there."

"Understood."

"And let me know if you learn anything about this male. We need to ID him. I'd like to speak to her alone, but if he's a boyfriend or similar, we may need to recruit him too."

"Understood. Exiting vehicle and approaching the building in character."

The Preceptor's helicopter landed at a small helipad on campus, just a few blocks from Sarah's location. There was a small airport north of town, but a local Order affiliate had access to an ROTC helipad that put him within walking distance of the Student Ecology Center.

When the Preceptor exited his quiet black helicopter, he was greeted by a dozen Initiates of Order in black suits and dark sunglasses with optical displays. Even with nearly identical suits and gear, the Midwestern or possibly Southern influence on the security detail composition was obvious to a trained eye. They were all broad-framed, tall, and mostly white males, although there was also one black male and a white female. The head of the security detail spoke with just a hint of Southern twang.

"Welcome to Southern Illinois, Preceptor. We're just a few blocks from your destination. Follow me."

The head of the detail walked alongside the Preceptor, leading the way across campus. Two of the Initiates followed closely behind as the rest spread out, scanning their surroundings and establishing a broad perimeter. There were a handful of students walking to or from classes, but no one seemed to notice the Preceptor and his detail.

The Preceptor was starting to admire the many species of trees on campus when he received a text message from the recruitment team leader.

Male is aware. They plan to meet after work. Male is leaving.

The Preceptor stopped, raising a hand to bring his security detail to a halt. "Aware" was common Order shorthand for anyone who was aware of the existence of Order or Anomalous phenomena. This was not a welcome development.

"Let me know when he's gone. I'll speak to her after he's gone but before she meets with--"

The team leader's voice on his earbud interrupted him

"They're driving away! She said she was staying, but she left with him. Should we pursue?"

The Preceptor clenched his fist. This wasn't going to be as easy as he'd hoped.

"No. We want her to come in voluntarily. A car chase won't help with that. Return to base and await further instructions."

The Preceptor closed the connection and sighed. With a few quick swipes on his tablet, he activated a backup plan that involved drone, satellite, and electronic surveillance. Then, he motioned for his protection detail to follow him back to the helicopter.

"Target is on the move. We're done here."

The Preceptor sat at a desk in St. Louis Keep's Emergency Command Center. It was a large room with a dozen steel desks, computers, and a blank white wall at the front of the room that served as a giant viewscreen. Since this wasn't an emergency, he hadn't bothered to assemble full support staffing of the ECC for his visit. Aside from six Initiates guarding the two main exits to the room, he was alone.

He stared at his computer, studying the latest reports in silence.

Sarah and her companion, a man named Taliesin Malek, had disappeared into the Shawnee National Forest. They had ditched Taliesin's car in St. Louis several hours ago and hadn't been seen since.

The Preceptor was lost in thought when his computer

chimed, notifying him of an incoming video chat.

Dr. Kendra Valda, Insight of Order.

The Preceptor routed the chat through the viewscreen at the front of the room. Her face appeared in front of him, larger than life, framed by glimpses of her favorite Icelandic telepresence room theme -- white marble walls, shelves full of ancient books, cerulean waves lapping along black sands behind her.

"Good evening, Preceptor."

"Good evening, Insight. To what do I owe the pleasure?"

The Insight smirked. "Our progress report? Have you forgotten scheduling it? I see that you're using video chat instead of telepresence room. How quaint."

"Oh. Yes, of course." The Preceptor took a deep breath, gathering his thoughts. "Do you and Toshi have any news on the scenarios? Is Favorable Anomalies still our only successful scenario?"

The warmth drained from the Insight's expression. "No news on that front, Preceptor. I would have told you immediately if there had been any changes. We can review the most recent changes to the scenarios if you'd like."

"No, that won't be necessary."

"Good. Is there anything else from my report that you'd like to review? There's a whole world out there beyond the climate crisis."

The Preceptor pulled up the Insight's most recent report on his monitor and started skimming. There were several serious new political and theological Anomalies that needed to be dealt with, and several technological advances that required approval, but none of it seemed particularly relevant to the climate crisis. After almost a minute of silence, the Insight cleared her throat.

"Is this a bad time, Truman? Should I call you back?"

"No, not at all. It's just been a busy day. Can you tell me more about the latest progress on Project Ark?"

The Insight's eyes lit up. "Are you asking because you're interested in space travel, or because you're becoming obsessed with the idea of the climate crisis crashing the whole system?"

"Both."

"Of course. Well, you'll be pleased to know that the latest round of warp drive proof-of-concept tests has been successful. The detailed results are still under review, but within the next few months, the new Alcubierre-White drive should be able to transport a significant payload at several times the speed of light for an extended period of time. We're reviewing both the technical details of the tests and the exceptionally complex challenges of gradually phasing this new technology into consensus reality. This is an exciting time for Order."

"Yes. That's why it caught my eye in your report. It's good to see some progress being made in the midst of all of this chaos."

"Agreed. Should we proceed with the first manned tests?"

"Yes. I--" The Preceptor paused, raising his hand to interrupt his previous train of thought. "Actually, no. Let's wait until the technology is ready for public consumption. The public deserves to see the first warp flight, just like they deserved to see the first moon landing."

"I see. Our pilots will be disappointed to hear that. But it does make a certain sense."

"They'll get their chance soon enough. In the meantime, put the full suite of Project Ark equipment on the first prototype."

A look of surprise flashed across the Insight's face.

"All of it?"

"Yes."

"This soon?"

"Yes."

The Insight's brow furrowed. "A full Project Ark suite would involve several billion dollars worth of additional equipment: experimental computers, experimental power systems, experimental biological samples. Everything that would be necessary to preserve the sum of human technical knowledge and recreate the human species on another planet in the event of a global catastrophe. And you want me to put all of this expensive equipment on our very first unmanned warp-capable prototype?"

"Yes. We need a Plan B, Kendra. And I'm not going to wait until 2049 to create it. Project Ark will ensure that if Order falls and human civilization is destroyed, the human species will endure in some form. Even if it's just as data on a hard drive hurtling through interstellar space."

"Okay. If anything goes wrong, though, we'll needlessly lose billions of dollars worth of equipment, on top of the billions spent on the warp drive prototype itself. I would highly recommend waiting a few years for the first fully-tested production model."

"I know the risks, Kendra. The reward of having a Plan B is well worth the risk of a few billion dollars."

"Okay. I'll have our team get to work on it immediately, then."

"Good. Is there anything else?"

"There are several other items in my report that require Level 5 action. Would you like to review those now?"

The Preceptor skimmed the report again.

"That won't be necessary. I'll reply in writing as needed."

"Understood." The Insight glanced over the Preceptor's shoulder at the empty Emergency Command Center. "Looks like you've got a busy night ahead of you."

"Hardly. But I need to focus on this Potential Favorable Anomaly. If Muhnugin's prophecy is accurate--"

"Bertram Muhnugin? THE Bertram Muhnugin?"

"Yes. If his prophecy is accurate, I should be meeting this PFA sometime in the next 36 to 48 hours."

"I see. I'll leave you to it, then. I look forward to hearing more about this PFA -- and your encounters with Muhnugin. Off the record, of course. For the Victory of Order."

"For the Victory of Order."

The Insight closed the connection. Her face and colorful Icelandic beach theme blinked out of sight. For a moment, the

Preceptor stared at the blank walk, lost in thought. Eventually, he returned his attention to his monitor and resumed his review of the latest reports.

◆ ◆ ◆

"Target acquired."

"You're sure it's her?"

"Yes. Primary target is on the move, on foot with three secondary targets."

"Good. Get me a visual. Try to bring her in voluntarily, but detain her if necessary. I don't want to lose her again."

"Understood."

The Preceptor turned on the large viewscreen at the front of the Emergency Command Center. The screen displayed a live aerial view of several city blocks with a green circle around four people near the center of the screen.

Something about the layout of the neighborhood looked very familiar.

"Target cluster now approaching Prometheus Plaza."

The Preceptor's pulse quickened. He felt a flash of intuition confirming his concerns about Sarah's destination. The International Prometheus Consortium kept coming up during the course of his search for solutions to the climate crisis. It couldn't be a coincidence. They clearly had some central role to play in the resolution of this crisis.

But there was something else going on here, too. He could feel it.

The Preceptor pulled up his global tactical map on his monitor. When he saw the big white crown symbol over St. Louis, he cursed under his breath.

The Sovereign.

What was the Sovereign doing in St. Louis? Was he at the International Prometheus Consortium headquarters? Did Sarah somehow know he was there? What was about to happen?

"Something's not right here. Bring the target in immediately."

"Understood."

The Preceptor zoomed in on the aerial view of Prometheus Plaza. There was a press conference in progress -- a temporary stage, a podium, and a small audience of reporters and spectators gathered in the plaza for some media event. He looked back down at his tactical display and noticed that the Sovereign was scheduled to speak at IPC today in the guise of his civilian persona -- Percival Sword, media mogul.

Sarah and her companions were already standing close to the stage. The Sovereign was standing at the podium.

Sarah started speaking.

The video feed went blank. The audio feed went silent. The Preceptor looked down at his monitor, puzzled. He checked his connection, but everything seemed to be working on his end. There just wasn't any data coming in from the remote site.

When the feed returned, the plaza was descending into chaos.

"--down! I repeat, target down! Primary and secondary targets are all down! Moving to intercept."

"Are they alive? Do you have them?"

"I--" The team leader paused. "It's alright, sir. It's White Diamond. They were intercepted by a White Diamond team before we could get to them. They've all been tranquilized and secured."

The Preceptor sighed. "At least they're alive. Provide any necessary backup for the White Diamond team, then pull out ASAP. Return to base. I'll contact the Guardian directly about the targets. Preceptor out."

"No. Absolutely not."

The Guardian's stern features loomed larger than life on the viewscreen of the Emergency Command Center. His cold grey eyes glared right through the Preceptor.

"Excuse me?"

"You heard me, Truman. You can't have Athraigh. And you definitely can't take the whole lot of them back to the Panopticon with you. Have you gone mad?"

"No." The Preceptor tapped on his golden headband. "Have you forgotten who you're speaking to? I am the Preceptor of Order. I am not making a request. I am issuing an order."

"An order that oversteps your authority. As Guardian of Order, I am tasked with safeguarding the integrity of Order's leadership structure. Athraigh is a direct threat to that structure. She sought out the Sovereign in his civilian life--"

"You're jumping to conclusions, Bill. She probably doesn't even know he's--"

"--and she attacked him in public."

"This wasn't an attack! She barely even spoke to him."

"There was something Anomalous going on here, Truman. I've never seen the Sovereign rattled like that. The man usually revels in lecturing people who disagree with him -- but after his encounter with Athraigh, he could barely speak. My men say the clouds parted and light shone down on Athraigh while she gave her little speech. Is she a Theological Anomaly?"

"Irrelevant."

"It's very relevant, Truman. Theological Anomalies are notoriously dangerous. Her Verwechseln score keeps going up and up. I don't know what she is, but she's extremely Anomalous."

"Yes. Which is why I need to speak with her. She's too Anomalous for us to bring her fully into the fold, but we need her on our side." The Preceptor paused, gathering his thoughts. "Look, Bill. I understand your concerns. I really do. And your decision to intervene today was the right decision. You were protecting the Sovereign from a potential threat. But now that the crisis is past, and the Sovereign is safe, Athraigh isn't your problem anymore."

"She's my problem if she poses a threat to you, Truman.

You're part of Order's leadership structure too. And the Panopticon is one of our most sensitive facilities. Most of the world doesn't even know that it exists."

"It's also one of our most secure facilities. And if she becomes violent during the course of the interview, you'll be fully justified in intervening. Until then, she doesn't fall under your authority anymore. I determine our response to all Anomalous individuals and phenomena. Period."

The Guardian shook his head.

"I don't like it, Truman. You're going too far with this PFA nonsense. You're playing a dangerous game."

"You don't have to like it. Just do it."

The Guardian's expression shifted subtly from a look of barely repressed anger to a more familiar look of begrudging acceptance.

"Will do. She's already in the air, so she'll be at the Panopticon slightly ahead of you. We'll keep her and the others in a holding cell until you're ready for her."

"Good. Preceptor out."

The Preceptor sighed. He hadn't even met this Sarah Athraigh woman yet, and she was already causing discord within the leadership structure of Order. Hopefully the post-extraction interview would go better than the botched effort at voluntary recruitment.

The Preceptor turned off the viewscreen and logged out of the computer. The St. Louis Emergency Command Center fell silent, empty of everyone but the Preceptor and a handful of guards. He dismissed them from their posts with a wave of his hand and headed toward the helicopter bay.

It was time to have a little chat with Sarah Athraigh.

CHAPTER 10

The elevator doors opened into a long, narrow hallway lined with several almost seamless doorways. The hall looked similar to many of the halls that the Preceptor walked through on a daily basis in the Panopticon and other parts of the massive underground Center that housed several of Order's key assets. The white ceiling, sky blue walls, and grass green floor were all glowing with a uniform luminescence that was bright enough to illuminate the entire hallway with the warmth of daylight but soft enough that looking at the panels felt comfortable and natural. On most days, the lighting and color scheme made a walk through the Center feel like a walk through an open meadow on a sunny spring day.

That wasn't how it felt today.

The hallway was narrower than what he was used to. It occurred to the Preceptor that he had almost never set foot in the holding cells or any other part of the Security wing. All new Initiates and most full-time security personnel spent a fair amount of time in Security for either guard duty or ongoing training exercises. But the Preceptor rarely met with Security staff in person, and the holding cells in this hallway were almost always empty.

Today, though, two of the cells were occupied. He walked down the hall and stopped in front of a cell that held a single highly Anomalous occupant.

Sarah Athraigh.

The Preceptor pulled out his tablet and reviewed Sarah's updated profile and strategic analysis one last time. Given her documented history of opposition to authority figures, she was unlikely to cooperate directly with Order even under the best of circumstances. The fact that she had been involuntarily extracted and transported to a maximum security facility reduced the chances of her voluntary cooperation to virtually zero.

Luckily, he didn't need her trust or even her cooperation. He just needed her to listen -- and to do her best to solve a problem that she was already trying to solve without the benefit of Order's considerable resources and superior analysis.

The Preceptor touched the wall next to the cell door and a white circle appeared, allowing him to open the door with a few quick gestures. The door slid open with a slight hiss, and the Preceptor stepped inside.

The cell was a standard ten by ten room with the same color scheme as the hallway -- blue walls, white ceiling, and green floor. Instead of the desk he was used to seeing in similar conference or telepresence rooms, there was a thin bed without legs built into the wall opposite the door.

An Initiate stood at attention next to the bed in full Champion field gear -- black body armor, assault rifle at high ready, thin black gloves, black helmet, big black headphones, and thick black goggles. There was always a platoon of Champions on duty at the Center due to the exceptional resistance to Anomalous activity provided by their unique gear and training. They didn't do routine guard duty in full gear, but it was standard protocol in the presence of a major Anomaly.

A young woman was lying in the bed attached to the wall. She was wearing black cargo pants, black hiking boots, and a simple forest green T-shirt. Her skin was pale, and her long black hair was pulled back in a ponytail. Her emerald green eyes were bright and alert even though she must still be emerging from the fog of Order's custom-made tranquilizers. Her arms, legs, and torso were held fast by transparent ceramic cuffs.

The Preceptor entered the room and stood in the doorway.

"Good morning, Sarah."

The bed that Sarah was lying on rotated into an upright position, then turned to face her toward the center of the room. Her eyes moved back and forth between the Preceptor and the guard, studying them both carefully before allowing her gaze to settle on the Preceptor's headband.

The Preceptor rarely even thought about his headband anymore. He wore it whenever he was working because it symbolized his connection to the Egregore, an entity that was both a creation of Order's collective consciousness and a guiding force behind Order's mission and operations. Lower-level Initiates often believed that the Egregore was just a poetic metaphor for Order's vast body of knowledge and insight into the world. But the Preceptor knew that it was something more -- a mystical yet very real presence in the world that spoke and acted through the Preceptor and the Initiates of Order. It wasn't something that he could speak with directly, but he felt its presence every time he received a burst of Preceptor's intuition.

As Sarah stared at the Eye of Providence on the center of the Preceptor's headband, his intuition told him that she understood something of the nature of the Egregore and his connection to it. She probably didn't understand it fully, but she could sense the Egregore's presence too.

"It's a nice touch, isn't it?" The Preceptor tapped the side of his headband lightly with his index finger, smiling warmly at Sarah. "You know nothing of our history, yet you already know what this is, don't you? I can see it in your eyes. Most of my staff will never perceive what you have already gleaned at a glance. Excellent."

The Preceptor touched the wall beside him, activating the control panel and releasing Sarah's restraints. She slid off of the bed and into a standing position, taking a moment to steady herself before placing her full weight on her feet.

The guard looked back and forth between the Preceptor and Sarah, rapidly assessing the threat level now that Sarah had been released from her restraints. The Preceptor waved him off dismissively with a slight smile.

"Don't worry, I'll take it from here." He motioned for Sarah to approach him. "Come with me. We have much to discuss."

For a moment, she simply stared at him quizzically. Rather than waiting for her to respond, he turned and walked out of the room. After a few seconds, he heard her footsteps trailing behind him. When they paused halfway down the hall, he turned to find Sarah studying the glowing walls.

"Transparent ceramics." He smiled broadly. "This technology is so advanced that I had to approve it personally. Our well-armed friend back there could unload his entire clip into this wall without penetrating it. The optical properties, however, would be affected."

They continued down the hall, passing several identical unmarked doors before stopping in front of one near the end of the hall. The Preceptor touched the wall beside the door, opening the cell with a few quick gestures.

When the door slid open, Sarah's eyes widened. The three companions who had been with her when she was extracted were all sitting around a transparent table, leaning in close and speaking to each other with hushed but urgent voices.

There were two men and one woman. One of the men was tall and athletic, with golden shoulder-length hair, bronze skin, and clear blue eyes. He was wearing a black superhero costume that looked equal parts practical and ridiculous, with a black latex body suit, a red deer logo on the chest, and a black utility belt with several buttoned and zippered pouches. The other man was more practically dressed in a light blue button-up shirt and navy blue cargo pants. He had disheveled orange hair, sky blue eyes, bold freckles, and a lanky frame. The woman was short, at most five feet tall, with long blond hair that floated freely in thin wisps across her cheeks and shoulders. She wore a T-shirt and skirt full of bright clashing colors and had a tablet computer strapped to a rainbow-colored armband on her right wrist.

As soon as the Preceptor and Sarah stepped into the

room, all three of them jumped to their feet.

"Sarah!"

The young woman, who the Preceptor recognized as an Anomalous Revolution militant named Patricia, ran up to Sarah and hugged her tightly. The two men, a somewhat famous Real Life Superhero named Hart and a suspected AR sympathizer named Taliesin, both looked deeply relieved to see that Sarah was alive and well. Taliesin followed Patricia to embrace Sarah, but Hart stopped short, crossing his arms over his chest and quietly glaring at the Preceptor.

The Preceptor maintained a relaxed posture, but kept his hands close to his concealed stun gun and firearm. He didn't expect any trouble from Hart, but it didn't hurt to be prepared.

"Do I detect hostility and posturing?" The Preceptor smirked, carefully studying Hart's body language and facial expression to confirm that he was not in fact an immediate threat. "You know, if it were up to the Guardian, you'd all be dead right now. Luckily, Bill's not the Preceptor. Not yet, anyway."

Patricia let go of Sarah and matched Hart's stance, crossing her arms and glaring at the Preceptor, her fist clenching so tightly that she started trembling slightly.

"This isn't funny! Are you the boss? Why didn't you kill us? Doesn't the Order like to kill Anomalies? You killed Addy!"

The Preceptor cringed, his head twisting slightly and his lips curling as he drew breath with an audible hiss. He would have preferred avoiding Patricia and the usual laundry list of grievances against Order that all AR militants seemed to enjoy carrying on about at length. But he knew that Sarah wouldn't even listen to him until she was reunited with her companions. The recent death of Patricia's AR contact in Chicago was apparently high on her laundry list, even though it had nothing to do with the far more urgent climate-related business he needed to discuss with Sarah.

Patricia had also triggered one of his few major pet peeves that he hadn't encountered since back in his days as an instructor.

"We are not called the Order. We are simply Order. We are currently the most advanced manifestation of Order, the most fundamental principle of reality. And it is through our efforts that humanity has evolved from a squalid mass of feuding peasants to a global empire of information technologists in under two centuries. Come, follow me."

The Preceptor turned around and left the room, walking down the hall toward the elevator. At first, he thought that he might have lost his audience. But after exchanging a few quiet words amongst themselves, they eventually followed him down the hall and into the elevator.

◆ ◆ ◆

"Welcome to the Panopticon."

The Preceptor stepped out of the elevator and beckoned for Sarah and her companions to follow.

Sarah and her companions stepped out of the elevator, looking around in wonder at the spherical room filled with colorful desks, transparent walkways, and the six foot diameter glowing crystal Eye at the center of it all. Several of the people working at the desks, including Dr. Bharati and Dr. Aino, stared openly at the new arrivals. But when Sarah sought to meet their gaze, they averted their eyes and returned to work.

The Preceptor led his guests across the walkway to stand around the Eye.

"The Eye uses a complex algorithm and vast amounts of data to create a real-time model of the integrity of consensus reality. Green indicates areas where all is going according to plan. Red indicates deviation. This includes satellite detection of Anomalous activity, meta-analysis of media and surveillance reports, and so on."

Sarah studied the globe carefully as the Preceptor continued.

"You have no idea how hard we work to keep this globe green. Every time Anomalous activity goes public somewhere, that region turns red. Every time a technological advance is made ahead of schedule, that region turns red. Sometimes a whole city turns red and we don't even know why. If we can't contain it, and it spreads, then consensus reality collapses, and the world as we know it ends."

Sarah crossed her arms over her chest, her attention still focused on the crystal sphere at the center of the room. He had the unsettling feeling that she might be getting intuitive flashes of information just like he did whenever he studied the Eye. Was the Egregore sending her information too, or was she receiving something from another source?

"Let me get this straight. Every time someone, some-where, does something that you didn't plan on, a red dot appears on this map?"

"Well, not every time, but yes." The Preceptor tapped on one of the red dots. "This little pocket of deviant consciousness has the potential to rewrite the whole consensus in its image. Maybe it's a political or religious faction that wants to take over the world. Maybe it's an invention that will destabilize the economy. Maybe it's some teenager who's using the power of his mind to burn down his school. Whatever it is, it is Anomalous. And we must contain and neutralize Anomalies. We must re-store Order before consensus reality corrupts beyond repair or dissolves entirely."

Sarah stepped up to the Preceptor, standing only a few inches away from him, her face twisting in anger.

"No. I don't buy it. I get it, but I don't buy it. Where's the freedom in your little plan? What if we like being freaks and thinking outside the box? What gives you the right to enforce your rigid blueprint on a living, breathing reality? The only thing more amazing than your technology is your arrogance."

The Preceptor waited for her to finish her self-righteous rant. He had heard and read plenty of similar rants from other Anomalous Revolution sympathizers, but somehow this one carried more sting because of the source. Sarah Athraigh was the Potential Favorable Anomaly who was supposed to change everything -- and yet here she was, ranting and raving like any other AR militant.

His Preceptor's intuition still told him that she was the key to solving this crisis. But that didn't mean he had to like it.

"Typical." The Preceptor smirked. "You people and your Anomalous Revolution. When architects design better bridges, you praise their ingenuity. When we design better societies, you condemn our hubris."

"Architects don't murder people."

The Preceptor's lips tightened and nostrils flared in anger. For several moments, he simply glared at Sarah. Eventually, he spoke.

"Everyone dies, Sarah. I make sure they die in the right order."

Sarah and her companions stared at the Preceptor in stunned silence. Before any of them could regain their composure, the Preceptor's expression brightened again. The first half of the tour clearly wasn't going well -- but he was confident that the second half would seal the deal.

"I have an idea! Let's go on a field trip! When it's over, you're free to go."

The Preceptor walked past Sarah and headed toward the elevator, gesturing for the others to follow. After a brief pause, he heard their footsteps following behind him -- until Hart spoke.

"What's the catch?"

The Preceptor paused next to the open elevator door. "Catch? There's no catch. Just listen to the rest of my story. Once you do, you're free to go."

Sarah, Taliesin, and Patricia followed the Preceptor into the elevator. Hart sighed, shaking his head and walking slowly down the walkway to join them.

The entrance to the Museum of Real Faery Tales consisted of two large oak doors with wrought iron hinges and thick iron rings for handles. Above the door, there was a roughly hewn oak sign with iron letters that read "MUSEUM OF REAL FAERY TALES." The Preceptor had always appreciated the fact that the doors looked entirely out of place, adding to the surreal aesthetic of the museum. When they reached the entrance, he pulled on one of the handles, opened the door, and stepped inside, gesturing for the others to follow.

The Museum of Real Faery Tales was a bit larger than a football field, with a thirty foot high ceiling and a cobblestone path that wound up and down dozens of aisles of various different types of displays. Some consisted of large touch screens that showed interactive slide shows or films. Others featured life-sized wax figures in period clothing ranging from medieval armor to Renaissance formal wear to modern business suits and black body armor.

The Preceptor started leading the group down one of the aisles, narrating as they walked.

"Since the dawn of history, human beings have encountered strange phenomena that defy all rational explanation. People lost in the woods encounter misshapen creatures that look almost human, but not quite. Ghosts of the dead haunt abandoned buildings or pay visits to the living. Wild-eyed madmen drink vials of toxic reagents or recite arcane incantations to develop supernatural powers over space and time, matter and energy."

The Preceptor stopped in front of the largest diorama in the museum -- the Horror of Wiltshire. A dozen immense men, large even by modern standards, were clad head to toe in shining steel armor and adorned in flowing black tabards, each with the bold white circle of Order on their chest. Most of these Initiates were wielding massive two-handed longswords. Two were armed with long, thin blades in one hand and a tower shield strapped to the other arm. An average-sized man was fully armored but had not drawn any weapons. Instead, he was reading from a book and shouting angrily at their opponent.

Their opponent was by far the most striking part of the diorama. The Horror of Wiltshire looked somewhat like a naked human being, but with the characteristic anatomical distortions of a full-blooded Fae Anomaly. It was almost twenty feet tall, and though it was currently hunched over to engage in combat with the men, it was still large enough to make them look like toddlers by comparison. Its ruddy green skin was thick and leathery, and its hairy arms were abnormally long, bulging with thick veiny muscles that would be uncharacteristic of such elongated features in a human. Its eyes, nose, and mouth were all disproportionately large, giving its blood-smeared face a crowded and inhuman look. Its eyes literally glowed with a crimson inner light, and its distended jaw was clenched around the helmeted head that it had just pulled loose from the body of one of the human Initiates that it held in its massive long-fingered hands. A stream of blood was squirting from the space where the man's head used to be, forever immortalized in motionless crimson wax that glistened wetly as though it were the real thing.

"Cool!"

Patricia looked up at the monster with a big smile and eyes wide with wonder. Sarah, Taliesin, and Hart looked up at it with more somber expressions. As they studied the creature, the Preceptor continued.

"This is real. This is why we must maintain Order. The Horror of Wiltshire killed all of those men, and it would have ravaged all of England if a second band of Order Initiates hadn't finished it off while it was still wounded."

Taliesin studied the statue of the creature.

"Is this a troll?"

"It was an unknown Faery creature. When it shambled into town and started devouring children, no one thought to ask its name."

"Surely it must have had a reason. Did someone destroy its habitat?"

The Preceptor laughed. He rarely had the opportunity

to speak with AR sympathizers in person. He had forgotten how readily they sympathized with even the most abhorrent of Anomalous phenomena. A vicious Fae Anomaly charges into a village in broad daylight and starts devouring children -- and the sympathizer's first impulse is to question whether or not someone destroyed the poor monster's habitat!

"Oh, there's always a reason. But does the reason make sense to a sane human mind? I've read your profile, Taliesin. I know that you communicate with Faeries during your rituals. You should know better than your friends here how dangerous some of these creatures are."

He paused for a moment, looking up at the Horror of Wiltshire with a cold, angry glare.

"They are Anomalous. Their psychology is alien, and they have the ability to warp reality itself with nothing more than the power of their minds. They're among the most dangerous Anomalies in the world."

The death of his own predecessor came to mind. Even after Order had all but banished the Fae from the civilized world, there were still pockets of Fae intrusion populated with beings powerful enough to kill a Preceptor. But he didn't want to give Sarah and her companions any ideas, so he didn't mention Derek's fate.

"So what does any of this have to do with us?" Sarah turned away from the huge statue to face the Preceptor. "Are you saying I'm one of these creatures?"

The Preceptor laughed. "No. You're a human female with as-yet-unidentified Anomalous qualities. I'd love to see you in one of my labs someday. In the meantime, this is just a warning. Don't be seduced by the simplistic romanticism of Anomalous Revolution."

"What about the simplistic tyranny of Order? You—"

The Preceptor cringed, his head twisting slightly as he held out a hand to interrupt Sarah. "Order is complex, not simple. And Order is aristocracy, not tyranny. We are the best and brightest of humanity united in the service of the evolution of human consciousness. We do not simply hunt human Anomalies like animals. We study them, we learn from them, and we declare some of them Prodigies who are expanding the boundaries of human potential."

"And what's the difference between a Prodigy and an Anomaly?"

"We have a rigorous protocol to determine the difference. But truthfully?" The Preceptor reached into his pocket and pulled out a gold pen. "This is the difference. The Sovereign and the Council of Order have entrusted the Preceptor with the duty of determining what is and is not a part of consensus reality. If I believe that humanity can handle the presence of an Anomaly without destroying itself or devolving into mass insanity, I will declare it to be a part of the consensus. This is true of both Anomalous human beings and Anomalous phenomena."

"So have you declared us part of the consensus? Or are you going to neutralize us too?"

The Preceptor paused. The standard modern Order protocols that he had helped develop would dictate that Sarah and her companions were too Anomalous to release from custody, and probably too Anomalous to exist at all. But the Potential Favorable Anomalous scenario indicated the need to take a different approach.

"In this case, it's not that simple. Sarah, walk with me for a moment. Patricia, why don't you and your friends go find the Anomalous technology exhibit."

"Ooh!" Patricia's eyes widened. "I knew there'd be a forbidden tech display! Is there a wax figure of Nikola Tesla? Let's go see!"

Patricia grabbed Taliesin and Hart's hands and started leading them away. Hart resisted at first, eyeing the Preceptor suspiciously. Sarah shrugged, and the Preceptor smiled.

"Don't worry, noble knight. I'll bring her back in one piece." He turned to Sarah, leaning in closer and lowering his voice. "He's a bit overbearing, isn't he? Not letting the womenfolk out of his sight?"

Hart glared silently at the Preceptor. Sarah smiled at Hart, catching his eyes and softening his expression with a warm look.

"I find it endearing." She touched Hart lightly on the shoulder. "I'll be fine, though, Hart. I'll be right back"

Hart sighed, shaking his head in resignation. Patricia tugged on his hand again and started pulling him down another aisle. Once Sarah and the Preceptor were alone, they started walking in a different direction.

"Do you know why I've brought you here, Sarah?"

"Climate change?"

The Preceptor smiled broadly. "I knew you were bright, Sarah. You're often quiet, but not for want of insight or lack of communication skills. You're constantly listening, watching, feeling — mindfully perceiving the situation with all senses and analyzing it from all angles. Yet you act with the intuitive spontaneity of a dancer or martial artist. With experience and training, you could join Order."

Sarah laughed. "Is that a compliment or an insult?"

"An observation."

The Preceptor stopped next to a large blank portion of the wall. He held his hand near the wall until a black circle appeared. With a few quick gestures, he pulled up a smaller two-dimensional version of the Eye's global display.

"Order is much more tenuous than most realize. The more sophisticated our models become, the more clear it becomes that climate change is an insurmountable crisis."

The Preceptor tapped a button on the screen, and a counter showing the current year appeared next to the globe. As the counter started advancing through the years, the colors on the globe fluctuated smoothly. After a couple of decades, the fluctuations became more sporadic. Around 2050, the entire globe flashed crimson and quickly faded to black.

"Too much is happening too quickly. Floods, droughts, wildfires, rising oceans, increasing frequency and severity of storms. Climate disasters displace tens of millions, which in turn leads to global instability, which in turn hastens human output of greenhouse gases."

The Preceptor tapped the screen again. The computer started displaying many of the other scenarios with unfavorable endings, each of them ending in similar flashes of crimson and black.

"I've tried everything. If we use force to stop all fossil fuel use today, the world quickly descends into violence and madness. If we don't, climate disasters worsen, ultimately forcing a global collapse. If we accelerate technological development, we're torn apart by Anomalies old and new. If we simply neutralize the majority of humanity, the climate recovers briefly, but the survivors are quickly torn apart by various psychological, social, and supernatural Anomalies. In short, consensus reality as we know it depends on a steady supply of cheap oil, but can't withstand the consequences of consuming it."

Scenario after scenario played out on the screen in front of them. For a long time, the two of them stared at the pulsing, flashing globe in silence. Eventually, Sarah was the first to speak.

"So you want us to do something about climate change?"

"Yes."

Sarah laughed. The Preceptor's smooth demeanor faltered for a moment, gawking at her slack-jawed as if she had suddenly gone insane. He had expected some form of resistance, but not such irreverence in the face of a global crisis.

"This isn't funny."

"No," Sarah's expression suddenly sank from amused to somber. "It's not funny. I just have a dark sense of humor. First a goddess tells me to do something about climate change. Then the head of some fascist global conspiracy tells me to do something about climate change. What's next, aliens?"

"Fascist?" The Preceptor cringed, clenching his fists for a moment before resuming his commanding composure. "One of my predecessors personally led the effort to neutralize the Nazi Anomaly. I realize the moral dilemmas inherent in my line of work, Sarah, but we are not fascists."

"Then what are you?" She pointed at the glowing globe displayed on the wall. "This is all well and good, but you know that I won't work for you, right? That I would never work for someone who blackbags or assassinates everyone who disagrees with their little plan for a New World Order?"

The Preceptor smirked. The conversation was getting back on track. He had fully expected her to reject any sort of direct cooperation and had prepared for their meeting accordingly.

"Oh, yes, I know. It's all right here."

With a few quick gestures, the Preceptor pulled up a new display that featured a photo of Sarah accompanied by several paragraphs of text. He scrolled through the profile to display more photos of Sarah and paragraph after paragraph of detailed analysis, including a timeline of her life and a full psychological profile.

"Early self-reliance due to orphan status, conscious rejection of authority due to deviation from prescribed worldviews, Anomalous beliefs and abilities, strongly-worded recommendation for neutralization. These are not qualities that we look for in our Initiates. Luckily, we can design missions that don't require the conscious cooperation of the participants." With a few quick gestures, he pulled up another window with a different document, this one mostly text. "You're very devoted to your cause, Sarah. You're also a practical woman. When I put a million dollars in your bank account, you'll use it for the mission, regardless of the source. And now that you know I'm watching, you'll avoid any Anomalous activity that would jeopardize your mission. As long as you don't make any more Anomalous public spectacles that threaten to destabilize society, you're free to do whatever it takes to solve the problem."

Sarah's eyes widened. "A million dollars? No strings attached?"

"Yes. I've been looking for someone like you for over two years — a devoted climate activist with profound and as-yet-unquantified Anomalous qualities. Your defiant attitude is a vital part of the equation. You and your little band of friends over there may be the only wild card that can change the future."

"No pressure, right?"

The Preceptor laughed. "None at all."

Without a word, the Preceptor turned off the display on the wall and started walking, motioning for Sarah to follow. After a minute of walking, they found Patricia, Taliesin, and Hart standing in front of a scale model of Wardenclyffe Tower, the wireless telecommunications tower designed by Nikola Tesla. When Patricia saw the Preceptor approaching, her face twisted into an angry scowl.

"You!" She ran up to the Preceptor and stopped just short of him, pointing at him emphatically. "How could you do that to Tesla! You set electrical engineering back a century!"

The Preceptor smirked, holding his hands up in mock surrender. "Hey, don't look at me. I wasn't born yet. Order has started integrating his technologies. He was just a man ahead of his time."

Patricia crossed her arms, still glaring at the Preceptor. "You can't keep science on a leash forever!"

"I don't intend to. Not all science. Not forever." The Preceptor smiled warmly, opening his arms wide and turning slightly to face the entire group. "Congratulations! You're free to go. The elevator will take you up to the minimum security complex on the surface. Good luck!"

Without another word, the Preceptor turned away and started walking toward the exit.

As the elevator doors closed, the Preceptor breathed a sigh of relief. Dealing directly with Anomalous Revolution members and sympathizers was surprisingly taxing. They always came with a laundry list of grievances, and they never seemed to appreciate just how vital the work of Order was to the evolution of human consciousness and the advancement of human society.

But in this case, he knew that it would be well worth the effort. Even without his Preceptor's intuition, he would have known that Sarah was the Potential Favorable Anomaly he was looking for. Her disdain for Order and authority in general were off-putting, to say the least. But they were essential traits for the Favorable Anomaly scenario.

There was something about Sarah that was perfect for the crisis at hand. There was a certain quiet charisma to her. She said little, but spoke plainly, genuinely, and decisively. As a result, other Anomalous individuals and events were already starting to gather around her. More would soon follow. And her effortless devotion to resolving the climate crisis would surely channel all of that chaotic Anomalous energy in the right direction.

It had to. She had to. At this point, there were no other options. The Favorable Anomalies scenario was still the only scenario with a significant chance of survival for the human species -- and Sarah Athraigh was now at the center of it.

The elevator doors opened. The Preceptor stepped out into the Panopticon. As he walked up to the Eye, he took a deep breath in and out, staring at the colorful globe displayed on the massive crystal sphere before him.

He was back in his element -- and Sarah was back in hers. There was a certain frustration in knowing that she was outside of Order's direct control. He could only observe her, and possibly use a few covert strategies to nudge her in the right direction. But even so, he felt like he might finally be on track toward a decisive solution to the climate crisis.

CHAPTER 11

The Preceptor walked into the conference room and stood at the head of the clear oblong table. Dr. Aino, Dr. Bharati, and the eight other staff members present rose to their feet. The room was set to its default theme -- sky blue walls and a white ceiling that together created an abstract feeling of being somewhere pleasant outdoors.

The Preceptor motioned for everyone to be seated, then sat down at the head of the table.

"Good morning. I've called this meeting to discuss the Favorable Anomalies scenario and its implementation. Dr. Aino, please give us a very brief overview of your latest update."

"Yes, of course. Thank you, Preceptor."

Dr. Aino cleared his throat, glancing down at the notes on his tablet for a few seconds before continuing.

"The concept of this scenario is simple. We selectively introduce certain chaotic elements into the system, then assume that the chaos resolves in favor of Order. This is not entirely unusual, you see. There are many cases where the individuals seem to behave chaotically, yet a complex and somewhat predictable pattern emerges from their interactions. The challenge, in this case, is in the details. What chaos do we let in? What do we exclude? Too much chaos, or the wrong type of chaos, and the system disintegrates. Not enough chaos, and the outcome remains unchanged. Business continues as usual, and the system collapses due to the inevitable consequences of human-caused climate change."

The Preceptor nodded. "Yes. And you have news about the details?"

"Yes and no. Here, let me show you."

Dr. Aino tapped and swiped on his tablet to pull up a new display window. Each of the four walls of the conference room was filled with a large white box with pink borders that displayed the presentation from Dr. Aino's tablet. The display cycled through various graphs and charts interspersed with blocks of text as Dr. Aino continued his explanation.

"As you can see, this scenario relies on extensive modeling of many elements of the system, including a few new models that account for the role of Anomalous elements in changing the course of Order. In fact, it's mostly the models and the math talking here, to be honest, rather than any humans proposing solutions and seeing how they play out. The newly updated scenario uses more detailed analyses and modelling to confirm the initial indication that this is a viable resolution to the climate crisis. Survival, progress, and model confidence have all increased a bit as a result."

"And what are the models telling us?"

"Ah, yes. To make a long story short, the models are telling us that we must be gardeners, of sorts. This Potential Favorable Anomaly -- this Sarah Athraigh -- she is at the center of this scenario. She combines the key elements of broadly Anomalous traits, social disposition, and narrowly focused commitment to action on climate change. But she is not alone in the scenario. What the scenario requires is more of a plant guild -- several plants that grow well together and support each other in creating the desired results. The role of Order, then, is to plant a few Anomalous seeds, and perhaps to weed the garden. Observe the situation, and let certain Anomalous elements flourish, but weed out others if they appear."

"I see." The Preceptor paused, reflecting on Dr. Aino's words. "Do you have any more specific recommendations? Actionable solutions rather than generalities and metaphors?"

Dr. Aino shrugged. "There are no easy answers here, Preceptor. I do what I can with the data presented. But we are dealing with the Anomalous, you see, which by definition we don't fully understand. I can now tell you very precisely what inputs the system requires from the Anomalous elements in order to resolve the crisis. This means that we will be able to assess Athraigh's impact on the scenario as time progresses. But how exactly to secure the necessary inputs is uncertain. Maximize Athraigh's input on the specific issue of climate, I would say, and maximize her ability to mobilize other Anomalous elements. But we must minimize the tendency of those other elements to destabilize the system in other ways. It's a delicate balance, to be sure. Walking a tightrope in a strong wind, not knowing which way that wind will blow."

The Preceptor had been hoping for something more concrete from Dr. Aino, especially now that Sarah Athraigh was in play.

"Yes. Athraigh is already using the seed money to mobilize a new activist campaign of some sort. I'll need every department's assessment of this campaign as it progresses -- social impact, economic impact, climatic impact, compatibility with our own efforts, all of it. Which reminds me, Dr. Bharati. What's the latest news on the climate science front?"

Dr. Bharati looked down at her tablet, reviewing her notes.

"I wish I had better news to report, Preceptor. The more we analyze existing data and conduct new research, the worse the outlook becomes. Sea levels will rise more rapidly and irregularly than we predicted even a few months ago. The impacts of several feedback loops have been confirmed and quantified, and we've refined our ability to input the projection results from our climate models into the Eye's various economic and political models. There is still much uncertainty, but we can say with a very high degree of confidence that the warming and its consequences do in fact pose an existential threat to human civilization as we know it."

The Preceptor sighed. "Right. And the geoengineering?"

"We're conducting initial trials of several techniques, particularly stratospheric aerosols, ocean fertilization, and ambient air capture of carbon dioxide. If successful, these methods may slow the warming enough to buy us an extra decade before the projected collapse. But each intervention comes with its own set of risks and challenges which we are attempting to reduce through extensive small-scale testing and other field and laboratory research. Our most optimistic projections now assume a near-total transition away from fossil fuels coupled with extensive geoengineering. The geoengineering will be necessary to counteract the warming we cause during our decades of transition away from fossil fuels. But even in concert, these strategies will not produce the desired results until the tail end of the century."

"Right." The Preceptor stared down at his tablet, idly paging through Dr. Bharati's latest report on climate science and geoengineering. "That brings us to the economic interventions. Dr. Edmund, any news on that front?"

Dr. Edmund was a middle-aged man in a black suit with a red bow tie. He had gray eyes, pale skin, and short black hair with a few hints of gray. When the Preceptor spoke to him, he pushed away his tablet and replied without reviewing his notes.

"Not much, I'm afraid. We've put together a comprehensive economic response plan that includes several carbon taxes in both developed and developing nations along with other financial instruments intended to address the market failures associated with greenhouse gas emissions. These will allow us to maintain or elevate regional and global energy consumption levels and standard of living while still accelerating the global transition away from fossil fuels and optimizing land use for carbon sequestration. However, creating such a fundamental shift in the global economy, particularly the energy sector, will take decades. In other words, our market-based interventions will definitely accelerate the transition, but not rapidly enough to avert the 2050 crash indicated by the metamodel."

"Alright." The Preceptor sighed, pushing away his tablet and staring off into space. "Alright then. Does anyone else have any other new information or strategy proposals on the climate crisis and its resolution? Or are we stuck sitting around waiting for Athraigh to make the next move?"

There was a long pause. The Preceptor looked around the table, searching for answers. Most people were looking away or reviewing their notes. Dr. Aino shrugged again. Dr. Bharati shook her head and sighed.

"Alright, then. Push your staff to brainstorm new approaches. The Anomalous aren't the only ones who can think outside of the box. Keep me posted. This meeting is adjourned."

The Preceptor sat alone in the telepresence room waiting for the meeting to start. The floors, walls, and ceiling all glowed with a bright but warm white light. After a few seconds, the ouroboros symbol on the wall transformed into a solid black ring, then faded out. A new set of images faded in all around the Preceptor, replacing the blank fields of white. He now appeared to be sitting in a ten-foot by twenty-foot conference room. The floor, walls, and ceiling were made of seamless black marble with gold veins and gold trim.

Someone was sitting at the other end of the conference table. Dr. Crevan Berchthild, Catalyst of Order, was a slender man in his mid-thirties with short, spiked orange hair, bright green eyes, and pale skin. He was wearing a green button-up shirt and black slacks. As soon as he appeared on the screen, he bowed his head slightly.

"Good evening, Preceptor."

"Good morning, Catalyst. It's still early in the day here. How's the weather in Mumbai?"

"Unbearably hot, as usual. I haven't set foot outside of the Keep in weeks, though, so I've been missing out." He laughed. "Speaking of the heat, how's your global warming thing working out? Make any progress with that Favorable Anomaly scenario?"

"That's actually what I'm here to talk to you about."

"Good! I could use something nice and wholesome like global warming to work on right about now. Cleanse the palate after all of the wetwork I've been up to lately, know what I mean?" He laughed. "Don't get me wrong. I enjoy a good covert regime change campaign as much as anyone. It takes tremendous skill to pull it off properly, and the end results are so much more immediate and satisfying than most of our other social engineering efforts. But sometimes at the end of the day, I just want to unwind with a few warm and fuzzy anti-poverty programs and environmental projects, you know? Some feel-good philanthropy to remind me what it's all about."

The Preceptor smirked. "You may get the best of both worlds with this one."

"Oh?"

"Yes. I have two objectives for you. The first is definitely warm and fuzzy. Do whatever you can to boost the signal of whatever this Favorable Anomaly of ours is working on. Social networks, media releases, white papers, grassroots and astroturf activist support, all of it. Whatever it takes to put this campaign of hers on the map. Don't tweak the content, even if it seems a bit Anomalous for your tastes. Just boost the signal and maximize favorable exposure."

"Ah, yes. Make sure all of the hippies and freaks tune in to whatever treehugging meme Athraigh's pushing. Help her shift the relevant subcultures in a favorable direction. The bread and butter of enlightened social engineering. Consider it done."

"Good. Keep me posted on your progress."

"Gladly. And the second objective?"

"That one's a bit more tricky. I want you to start planning and implementing a psyops campaign against fossil fuel industry leadership, top stockholders, think tanks, and the like. Key economic and political players in the climate crisis. Push them to doubt the profitability of the industry for their one-year and five-year forecasts. Run interference on any efforts to shift public opinion in favor of fossil fuel infrastructure and consumption. If necessary, develop strategies to install new leadership more closely aligned with the goal of rapid transition away from fossil fuels."

The Catalyst blinked. His eyes widened.

"Whoa. I... did I hear that right? Psyops and regime change against the global fossil fuel industry?"

"Yes."

"You... do know that Order gets a significant portion of its operating funds and logistical support from the fossil fuel industry, either directly or indirectly, right? I don't know where we'd be right now without the support of all of those crusty old energy and mining oligarchs in--"

"I'm the Preceptor, Crevan. I'm well aware of both the potential and the inevitable consequences of what I'm proposing. I'm also aware of what the consequences are if climate change continues unabated. I've made my choice. We're doing this. Start doing all of the planning and preparation necessary for this to become actionable at a moment's notice."

"Right." The Catalyst paused, tapping his fingers on his desk. He glanced anxiously back and forth between his tablet and some empty point in space to his side, lost in thought. "I'll see what I can do. Let's start with the basics, shall we? Run some interference, manufacture some doubt, get a few operatives in place, make those oligarchs sweat a little. Hopefully we can shift a few key players and realign the whole herd without having to decap any big institutions. No need to shoot ourselves in the foot if we don't have to."

"Yes." The Preceptor nodded. "The metamodel still says that Order can't single-handedly shift global society away from fossil fuel consumption in time to avert a global crash. But I'm hoping that as Athraigh's efforts progress, that will change. When it does, we need to be ready. That includes having plans in place to take swift action against the fossil fuel industry if necessary. I hope it doesn't come to that, but Order will prevail, with or without them."

"I..." The Catalyst raised a finger, as if to object, then lowered it slowly as he changed his mind. "I suppose there's no harm in plans. Hell, we have serious plans for what to do in the event of a zombie pandemic or alien invasion. We may as well have plans for a decap attack against the fossil fuel industry. Why not?"

"Exactly." The Preceptor smiled. "Let me know when you have something ready for my review."

"Definitely. And in the meantime, just give Athraigh the Catalyst Bump?"

"Yes. I've got other people watching her in case any other interventions are needed. But as far as social engineering goes, all we need right now is to boost her signal. She's the keynote. As long as some of the other Anomalous elements fall in line with whatever she's offering, we'll make it through this in one piece."

"Excellent! I'll get to it. Is there anything else we need to discuss today?"

"No, not today. I'll send more details as needed. Preceptor out."

The Preceptor sat at his desk in the Panopticon, reviewing the latest climate research summary sent to him by Dr. Bharati. In addition to the publicly available research, the report included her projections on the impact of current and near-future geoengineering efforts on various climate models and projections, with some notes from Dr. Edmund about the economics involved.

Geoengineering was likely to have a substantial, but not game-changing, impact on the climate crisis. If Order used all available and soon-to-be available technological interventions, and they all went according to plan, the warming trend could be slowed considerably. But the more dramatic the intervention, the greater the risk of implementation errors or unforeseen side effects that could be as bad as the original warming, if not worse. The only technological intervention that would resolve the crisis with any degree of certainty was deceptively simple: immediately cease all fossil fuel emissions and make land use changes to reduce agricultural emissions and sequester additional carbon. However, the economic, psychological, and sociological models all clearly indicated that this instantaneous shift in emissions patterns was impossible without either causing or being caused by massive social upheaval and its associated catastrophic death toll.

In other words, geoengineering would only delay the inevitable. Sooner or later, the system was still going to crash. The only question remaining was how quickly and brutally it would all come crashing down.

The Preceptor was so immersed in his reading material that he almost didn't notice when his computer chimed, notifying him of an incoming video chat. After a few seconds, he glanced up at the corner of his monitor to see who was calling.

It was the Sovereign.

An unscheduled video chat from the Sovereign was highly unusual. They often sent each other messages and had periodic video chats and face-to-face meetings. But the Sovereign's civilian life as a successful businessman and media mogul kept him very busy. He had seldom if ever made any unscheduled contact like this before.

The Preceptor answered the call.

"Good evening, Sovereign."

"Good evening, Preceptor. What's on your schedule for the rest of the night?"

"I have a few more staff reports to review, then I'll be meeting with the Insight via telepresence to review recent developments in the biotech--"

"Good. Clear your schedule, Truman. Meet me at Providence Catalysis immediately. I'm already en route, but you can beat me there if you leave now."

The Preceptor's pulse quickened.

"Is something wrong? I--"

"We'll talk about it when we get there. Sovereign out."

The video chat window closed. The Preceptor stared at

his monitor blankly for a moment, then rose to his feet suddenly and headed for the elevator.

Whatever this was all about, he didn't want to be late.

CHAPTER 12

The Sovereign's large black helicopter descended swiftly from the overcast sky, landing almost silently at the center of the cobblestone helipad near the main entrance of Providence Catalysis. The Preceptor stood near the edge of the helipad, glancing back and forth between the arriving aircraft and the marble archangel statues that lined the main path into the building. When the Sovereign emerged from his helicopter, he motioned for the Preceptor to follow him down a smaller side path that wound its way behind the building through the topiary garden.

For nearly a minute, the two men walked the cobblestone path together in silence. The Sovereign was famously loquacious in his public life, so the Preceptor found this long wordless pause very unusual.

Eventually, the Sovereign spoke.

"Truman."

"Yes, Sovereign."

"I've been reviewing your response to anthropogenic global warming."

The Preceptor paused.

"Oh?"

"Yes. You've been devoting considerable resources to it, haven't you?"

"Yes. It's currently the only crisis that definitely crashes the entire system. There are a few other vital concerns, of course, but system collapse due to climate change is all but certain without considerable intervention."

"Right. About that." The Sovereign stopped in place, pulling out his tablet. "I'd like you to take a look at this scenario I've been working on. It's a solution to the so-called climate crisis that seems to have escaped your attention."

The Preceptor looked at the Sovereign's tablet. It displayed a small two-dimensional version of the global metamodel that he usually viewed on the Eye.

"You've been working on metamodel scenarios?"

"Yes. I'm not as familiar with the models as you are, but I consulted with Dr. Aino in the creation of this new scenario."

"I see."

The Preceptor looked at the Sovereign's new scenario. The scenario was labeled "Consolidate and Rightsize." When the Preceptor tapped on the button to run the scenario, it cycled through to the end of the century ten times in rapid succession. The entire globe turned various shades of orange and red during the middle of the century, but by the end of the century, it was almost entirely green. Survival, progress, and confidence ratings were all above ninety percent for every run of the scenario.

The Preceptor felt his pulse quicken. At a glance, this seemed like an even better solution than the Favorable Anomalies scenario. This could change everything.

"Impressive. How does it work?"

"It just involves a few tweaks to the success parameters. Take a look at the details."

With a few taps and swipes, the Preceptor started skimming the technical details of the scenario. Most of it looked so similar to the Standard scenario that it took a moment for him to even notice the main difference.

When he did, his heart sank.

"Population. You've changed the limits on depopulation."

"Yes. It was simple, really." The Sovereign smiled. "All of your scenarios seem to assume that for Order to endure, most of humanity must survive. But the data doesn't support that conclusion! Quite the contrary. There are several relatively simple and elegant solutions that involve dramatic reductions in population. As long as our allied institutions retain central control of key economic and political resources, we can transition successfully to much lower human population levels. In this scenario, standard of living and ecological footprint both see dramatic improvements by the end of the century."

The Preceptor studied the numbers in silence. Everything that the Sovereign said was true. Under the Sovereign's new scenario, the climate crisis would be resolved -- and by the end of the century, the majority of people around the world would live very comfortable and happy lives with minimal environmental impact.

But over ninety percent of humanity would die in the process.

Seven billion deaths were projected in a single twenty-year span from 2040 to 2060. By the end of the century, the population was projected to stabilize naturally at approximately 625 million, as compared to the 8 billion plus alive today. Previous scenarios had automatically considered such rapid depopulation to be a sign of scenario failure. The Sovereign's scenario considered rapid depopulation to be an acceptable part of a successful outcome as long as global society remained under Order's control and humanity advanced toward its development goals.

The Preceptor stared at the Sovereign's tablet blankly for a while before responding.

"You can't be serious."

"Of course I am!" The Sovereign laughed. "Are you seriously going to object to this scenario? The death toll is unfortunate, of course. But we're not responsible for most of it. It's mostly due to the inevitable conflict and economic instability that occurs when billions of impoverished people are displaced from their homes by the effects of global warming. But the resulting wars, famines, and declining birth rates solve that problem almost as rapidly as it arises. With proper planning, the result is a small population of overachieving survivors who are highly intelligent, resilient, and affluent. Honestly, global society becomes much more manageable once we're rid of a few billion takers! It'll be a rough couple of decades, but global warming is doing us a favor in the long run."

The Preceptor handed the tablet back to the Sovereign. He stared off into the distance, contemplating what the Sovereign and his new scenario were telling him. As Preceptor, he was used to making difficult choices. Choices that would affect the course of nations. Choices that would in a very real sense alter the fates of millions of people. But this was beyond any choice he'd been asked to make before.

Seven billion lives, gone in a single generation. It was almost unthinkable.

But would it work?

The Preceptor felt a dizzying rush as intuitive information about the situation flooded his consciousness. This Consolidate and Rightsize scenario did have the potential to succeed, if the loss of over seven billion people could even be described as a success. But the Favorable Anomalies scenario also still had the potential to succeed. It involved far fewer deaths, but much greater Anomalous activity and overall uncertainty.

He would have to choose between them.

"Truman? Are you still with me?"

"Yes. Actually, no." He turned to face the Sovereign with a cold glare. "No, I'm not with you. This new scenario of yours is outrageous. The Favorable Anomaly scenario resolves the crisis with dramatically fewer casualties. And besides, your role in Order is to determine the broad strokes vision of the organization, not micro-manage its implementation. Favorable Anomalies is still the best solution."

The Sovereign's usual cheerful expression and casually charming manner suddenly dropped away, replaced by a look of utter contempt and a face flushed with barely suppressed rage.

"Now listen here, Truman. I am the Sovereign of Order. When I--"

"And I am the Preceptor of Order."

"Yes, you are the Preceptor of Order, sworn to serve the

will of the Council of Order. So when I say we're going with this scenario, we're going with it. Period."

"Your scenario runs contrary to the mission of Order. Seven billion dead in a single generation. I will find another way."

"The mission of Order is whatever the hell I say it is!"

"The full Council crafts the mission of Order, not the Sovereign alone."

"Then take it up with the Council!"

"I will."

The Sovereign took a deep breath and sighed. As soon as he regained his composure, the familiar look of confidence and charm returned just as quickly as it had left.

"I've already discussed it with them, Truman. Seven billion deaths is compatible with the mission of Order as long as the outcome for Order is favorable. And plotting a decapitation attack against the fossil fuel industry as a solution to the climate crisis is not compatible with the mission of Order. Those are two policy-level determinations that are very much within my authority to make -- and I've made them. And the Council agrees. You can tweak the details of your scenarios however you want, but what I'm telling you is that this crusade of yours is over. Find solutions that don't involve sacrificing our core alliances and objectives, even if that means seven billion maladapted humans die. Order will prevail without them."

Before the Preceptor could respond, the Sovereign turned and walked away. The Preceptor watched him recede down the cobblestone path, step into his waiting helicopter, and disappear almost silently into the overcast sky.

When the Sovereign's aircraft was finally out of sight, the Preceptor pulled out his tablet and started a group chat with his senior staff.

Emergency confidential meeting in the Panopticon conference room tomorrow at 0800. Be prepared to discuss details of the Favorable Anomalies scenario at length.

The Preceptor walked back down the cobblestone path

to the helipad and sent a message to his crew requesting immediate pickup. As he waited for his helicopter to arrive, he took a long look at the four marble archangel statues that lined the path to the main entrance of Providence Catalysis.

Was he walking the path of Order? Or was he straying from it?

Only time would tell.

CHAPTER 13

The Preceptor walked into the conference room and stood at the head of the clear oblong table. Dr. Aino, Dr. Bharati, and the six other staff members present rose to their feet. The room was set to a cathedral theme -- specifically, the Cathedral Church of St. Brigid, Kildare. The theme was designed so that they seemed to be holding their meeting in the church's central crossing. The grey stone walls of the historic Irish cathedral rose all around them, terminating in pointed arches and broad oaken rafters high overhead. The conference table was positioned so that the chancel and altar were behind the Preceptor while the rest of the table was closer to the nave and its tidy rows of wooden seating for the laity. The many stained-glass windows suffused the entire church with soft, colorful light, the brightest of which was shining from the three main windows over the altar behind the Preceptor.

After the Preceptor entered, the door closed, smoothing away the odd rectangular gap and completing their immersion in the remote cathedral setting. The Preceptor motioned for everyone to be seated, then sat down at the head of the table.

"Good morning. I've called this meeting to discuss the latest developments with our metamodel scenarios. Have all of you had a chance to review my summary of the Sovereign's proposed scenario?"

The room fell silent. Everyone looked down at their tablets or off into the distance. There were a few audible sighs and the sounds of people shuffling in their seats.

"I'll take that as a yes. You understand, then, how grave the situation is. Seven billion dead is now considered a successful outcome as long as Order endures. The Sovereign himself has made this eminently clear to me. However, we still have options."

The Preceptor picked up his tablet. With a few quick taps and swipes, he made four identical chalkboards appear on the four sides of the conference room. The virtual chalkboards were fairly convincing, but somehow seemed slightly less realistic than the rest of the cathedral. Each virtual chalkboard started looping through a series of different metamodel scenarios -- maps of the world drawn in very fine detail with brightly colored virtual chalk.

"I've modified the parameters of all scenarios in accordance with the Sovereign's new mandate. Seven billion deaths is no longer considered a deal breaker. But it's also not a necessity. If we can achieve similar or better results for Order without those casualties, then the Favorable Anomalies scenario will be considered more successful. And we can do it. I know it."

The Preceptor tapped on his tablet. All of the chalkboards switched to display a single familiar scenario.

"Favorable Anomalies is still our preferred scenario. It achieves the best outcome with the lowest number of casualties. However, it's also the most difficult scenario to manage. It's a high-risk scenario. It threatens Order's key alliance with the fossil fuel industry, and it relies primarily on Anomalous elements that are almost entirely beyond our control. Dr. Aino, can you give me a status update on our progress with this scenario?"

"I will do my best, Preceptor. My specialty is the models, you see, not the real world data. But of course, they are related. I have been working with the Insight and the Catalyst to understand what is happening out in the field and how it affects the progress of various scenarios."

"Yes. And how is Favorable Anomalies progressing?"

"It's perhaps a bit too early to be certain. Even Anomalous shifts in global consciousness take time, it seems. But we're developing some sense of what Athraigh's team is up to and what the long-term effects will be."

"And?"

"She may benefit from an intervention, Preceptor. She is creating waves with a new program called Green Goes Global which mobilizes grassroots climate activists in new and interesting ways. We are studying her methods to see if we can perhaps reverse engineer them and redeploy them among the more well-funded nonprofits. But she is still somewhat limited in her reach. Big waves in a small pool, I would say. She is affecting deep change, but the pool needs to be bigger."

"That makes sense. Do you have any suggestions for interventions?"

"Yes. The Catalyst is developing a more detailed list of specific interventions. That is more of his specialty. Generally speaking, we must boost her access to institutional support and influence. She's currently traveling to meet a famous musician, which might expand her reach into a pop cultural context. We expect her popular influence to grow rapidly in the coming weeks. She may actually be dangerous in that regard, to be honest. Very charismatic. But her weakest area so far is her lack of interface with the more structured elements of society. Large institutions, powerful individuals, and so on. She is more of a rebel, unfamiliar with the nuances of interacting with institutional power. If she does not interface soon, an antagonistic relationship will develop, and she will be stuck in a small pool."

"That makes sense. I've had that impression of her from the beginning. I look forward to seeing more details from the Catalyst." He turned to Dr. Bharati. "Dr. Bharati, what do you think of this Green Goes Global project? Is it actually going to have any impact on human-caused climate change?"

"The social scientists may have a better answer for you, Preceptor." Dr Bharati leaned back in her chair with a sigh. "Solving this problem is fairly simple from an earth sciences perspective. Rapidly reduce greenhouse gas emissions and use various methods of carbon capture and storage to draw down excess greenhouse gases from the atmosphere. We have the necessary knowledge and technology. What we lack is the political will."

"Yes, true. Assume that the Green Goes Global strategy is wildly successful, though. What would be the climate impacts?"

"Considerable." Dr. Bharati looked at her tablet, pulling up the Green Goes Global summary to refresh her memory. "They're taking a very broad-based approach here. They consider the carbon footprint of individuals, small businesses, large businesses, public institutions, and so on. They use a network of local grassroots activists and consultants to assess how individuals and groups in each region can reduce their carbon footprint. They discuss a variety of specific, practical, readily implementable solutions, which is important. The impact will be considerable."

"Yes. Considerable. But will it be enough?"

"Their approach will accelerate progress in certain areas of emissions reduction tremendously. However, as Dr. Aino has mentioned, they lack robust institutional support. Achieving their zero emissions goal will likely require dramatic shifts in federal policy and international agreements. This will be necessary to respond to one of our greatest concerns from a climate science perspective: the looming threat of 'carbon bombs.'"

Dr. Bharati pulled up a report on her tablet and displayed it on the walls of the conference room. The four virtual chalkboards disappeared, replaced by four simple floating white squares of similar size. Each square displayed the same image: a map of the world with a dozen large red dots and several dozen smaller orange dots.

"These are the world's most emissions-heavy projects that are currently or nearly in operation. There is no known way to avert catastrophic climate change unless we stop the majority of these projects, or find some technological way to drawn down tremendous quantities of greenhouse gases from the atmosphere within the next few years. And incremental reform at the local or regional level doesn't seem likely to defuse these so-called carbon bombs because they currently enjoy powerful governmental and corporate support. But that is a question for the social scientists. I can only tell you that from a climate science perspective, the carbon bombs must be defused. Otherwise, we will have multiple degrees Celsius of warming this century."

The Preceptor sighed. Most of the larger red "carbon bombs" were readily identifiable to him at a glance: coal mining in China; coal exports in Australia, Indonesia, and the United States; Arctic oil drilling; Canadian tar sands. These were all projects that had a massive carbon footprint, but also strong support from the International Prometheus Consortium and its patrons in the fossil fuel industry.

Stopping one of them would be difficult, but achievable. Stopping most or all of them simultaneously would be virtually impossible.

"I see."

The Preceptor stared at the map in silence. As he started receiving intuitive information about the various fossil fuels projects it represented, a thought occurred to him.

"Dr. Aino, I have a new priority for you."

"Oh? What is it, Preceptor?"

"We've made great progress in our analysis of the Favorable Anomalies scenario. What I need for you to do now is delegate the remaining details to other staff and focus on analyzing the Sovereign's scenario and its implications."

The Preceptor pulled up the Sovereign's scenario on his tablet. The abstract rectangles on the four walls were replaced with virtual chalkboards displaying the global scenario map.

"We seem to have a--" He paused, searching for a diplomatic way of describing his disagreement with the Sovereign. "A difference of opinion emerging among the leadership of Order. The Sovereign is convinced that the death of seven billion people is a perfectly acceptable solution to the climate crisis. Based on certain details of my conversation with him, I strongly suspect that the Catalyst agrees with him. I don't know yet where the Insight stands, but I assume the Guardian stands with the Sovereign. He's never been a fan of Favorable Anomalies."

The Preceptor used his tablet to close the scenario displays. The four virtual chalkboards disappeared.

"I, on the other hand, do not see such a high death toll as an acceptable outcome. I would rather place all of Order at risk than sit quietly by while Order presides over the preventable deaths of seven billion people. Make no mistake: if that's the only way to preserve Order, then so be it. Order will prevail. But I refuse to accept that as a first choice. We will pursue the Favorable Anomalies scenario -- and if we fail, we'll do what needs to be done to preserve Order."

The Preceptor turned to Dr. Aino. "I need you to use the metamodel to poke holes in the Sovereign's scenario. If we can't convince them with a moral argument, then let's convince them with the data. Would Order really survive if that many people died that quickly? If we can prove that consensus reality can't handle that rapid of a downsizing of the human population, then Favorable Anomalies is once again our one and only viable solution to the climate crisis."

Dr. Aino nodded. "Very insightful, Preceptor. This is the way to respond to the Sovereign's scenario. I will work on this right away."

"Good. I also need to see some modeling of scenarios in which Order itself decreases its own reliance on economic and political support from the fossil fuel industry. The big oil and coal majors helped make Order what it is today. But for better or worse, some combination of our own actions and Anomalous activity may disrupt the whole industry and our access to it. We need to prepare for that eventuality."

"Yes. It will be difficult, Preceptor. We will have to think outside of the box, you see, and use the Anomalous elements to our best advantage. It will be a difficult process to model, Preceptor. But I will do what I can."

"Thank you, Toshi."

The Preceptor looked around the table at the handful of

people gathered in the conference room. They rarely spent any off-duty time together, but along with a few other top-level staff, they had all spent countless work hours together. Much of that time in recent months had been spent reviewing and acting on countless details of Order's response to the climate crisis. They were all starting to look a bit overworked and discouraged -- and he wondered if he was too.

He took a deep breath and let it out slowly before continuing.

"Regardless of what happens from this point forward, we're entering into a difficult time for Order. As the crisis worsens, internal divisions within Order may deepen. But I'm confident that this team will always pull together like it has in recent months and produce the very best analysis and solutions on the planet. Thank you all for your service. For the Victory of Order."

The Preceptor sat at his desk in the Panopticon, reviewing Dr. Aino's assessment of Sarah Athraigh's progress in fulfilling the parameters of the Favorable Anomalies scenario. He could already think of a few people off the top of his head who might be able to help Sarah and her companions make inroads into various institutional structures relevant to their interests and talents. The question was when and how exactly to make the introductions.

As he was skimming over the personality profiles of various candidates, a thought occurred to him. With a few quick swipes and taps on his screen, he opened an audio chat with the Catalyst.

"Good evening, Catalyst."

"Good afternoon, Preceptor. I wasn't expecting you. I didn't miss a check-in, did I?"

"Not at all, Crevan."

"Good. How can I help you, then?"

"I'm calling about the event tomorrow at Providence Catalysis. The annual Foundation fundraiser."

"Yes! You'll still be attending, won't you? It's just a formality, of course, but--"

"Yes. In fact, I'd like to bring along a few extra guests."

"Oh? Would you like me to take care of the background checks and handle transportation?"

"No, that's alright. I'll take care of it. I just wanted to keep you in the loop."

"Oh." The Catalyst paused. "Send me the details, then?"

"Yes. You'll have the flight plan information in the morning."

"Thank you. Anything else?"

"No, that's it. Preceptor out."

The Preceptor closed the audio chat and opened a text chat with the Panopticon's director of transportation.

Arrange transport for Sarah Athraigh and four guests to Providence Catalysis fundraiser.

CHAPTER 14

The Preceptor emerged from a nearly silent black helicopter idling on a cobblestone helipad near the main entrance to Providence Catalysis. He was dressed in his formal wear -- a black evening tailcoat, white shirt and bow tie, a low-cut white waistcoat, and a golden sash with a bold embroidered black "O" with a white center. A handsome young man in an elegant white tuxedo with a black bow tie and white gloves greeted him at the edge of the helipad.

"Welcome, Preceptor. The festivities have already commenced. Would you like me to escort you to the private room you requested?"

"Yes."

The attendant led the Preceptor through the front doors of the colonial-era mansion. Several other guests had already arrived and were congregating in the dining room and lounges. The teal walls were framed in white wood trim and adorned with over a dozen life-size portrait paintings of prominent Initiates of Order -- former Sovereigns, Preceptors, Insights, Guardians, and Catalysts dressed in period clothing ranging from colonial era to the present day.

"This way, Preceptor."

The Preceptor followed the attendant upstairs. They walked down a long hallway, stopping at the second doorway on the right. The attendant gestured toward the doorway with a bow, then returned downstairs.

The room was relatively small, with enough space for a simple wooden office desk and an ornate wooden table with eight matching chairs. Two of the seats were empty. Five of the other seats were filled with familiar faces: Dr. Aino, Dr. Bharati, and three of Dr. Bharati's staff. The sixth person, however, was someone he had only seen before on TV and in her profile in Order's database.

Congresswoman Irene O'Neill was a woman in her mid to late thirties with brown hair, brown eyes, a slightly round face, and a full figure. Her features were smooth and youthful, but her expression was serious, and her eyes shone with a warm intelligence that studied the people around her with a judicious balance of human warmth and careful calculation. She was wearing a charcoal grey suit jacket and slacks with a white blouse and her hair up in a ponytail.

Everyone rose to their feet when the Preceptor entered the room.

"Welcome!" The Preceptor shook the Congresswoman's hand and gestured for everyone to be seated, taking a seat at the head of the table. "Congresswoman O'Neill, I presume?"

"Yes. You can call me Irene."

"Thank you, Irene. Truman Stuart, Preceptor of Order. You can call me Preceptor or Truman. How familiar are you with the work of Order?"

"Not very. I only know what I've heard in rumors from fellow members of Congress and some of my other contacts in D.C."

"Good. Our existence is no secret in political circles, but we do prefer to exercise a bit of discretion about the details. The important thing for you to know is that we're here to help. You were recently appointed to the Joint Select Committee on Climate Change Mitigation and Readiness, yes?"

Irene nodded. "Yes. I'm looking forward to the opportunity to do some serious work on climate policy. The more I learn about the climate crisis and how it affects my constituents, the more I want to make climate policy and advocacy my primary focus."

"Good. Have you had a chance to review the report I prepared about Order's response to the climate crisis?"

"Yes, I was just asking your staff a few questions about the different scenarios." She stared down at the binder full of information that the Preceptor and his staff had prepared for her. "I don't know which is more unsettling -- the severity of the climate crisis or the severity of your proposed solutions."

The Preceptor nodded. "I fully expected you to find both unsettling. Our objective here is to make the best of a very difficult situation. As you can see, our preference is for the scenario that results in the fewest casualties and the quickest resolution to the climate crisis."

"The Favorable Anomalies scenario."

"Yes."

Irene paged through the binder idly, reviewing a few key sections while they spoke. "I take it you've invited me here to help with this scenario in some way?"

"Yes. Have you had time to review the personal profiles at the end of the report?"

"Only just barely. I arrived here about an hour ago."

"Yes. Well, you can take the binder with you, along with a digital copy that my staff will provide to you. This information is, of course, confidential -- not to be shared with anyone outside of Order."

"Understood."

"Good. I've invited you here today to speak with our best lead for the Favorable Anomalies scenario: Sarah Athraigh. Sarah is an accomplished activist and experienced community organizer, but she needs to connect with contacts who have more experience and connections in public policy, especially at the federal level. Anything that you can do to help her in her efforts to respond to the climate crisis would be greatly appreciated." He looked down at his tablet and noticed a new notification from his director of transportation. "In fact, I believe she's arriving now. If you'll excuse me, I'd like to greet her and her party."

"Of course. I look forward to meeting her."

"Yes. Thank you. I'll be back shortly."

The Preceptor left the room, retracing his steps down the hallway and back to the first floor. More guests had already arrived in the short span of time he'd spent upstairs. He didn't see Sarah yet, so he accepted a glass of wine offered by one of the servers in white tuxedos and quietly watched the crowd.

For the most part, the Preceptor felt inspired by the sight of the growing number of party guests arriving at Providence Catalysis. Prominent political leaders, business leaders, philanthropists, scientists, engineers, and other visionary change-makers were all gathering here today to show their support for Order's public foundation, the Foundation for the Advancement of the Initiation of a Transcendent Humanity. Through their individual efforts, and through the more discreet and methodical behind-the-scenes operations of Order, they were advancing human knowledge, prosperity, and technological achievement more rapidly than at any previous point in human history.

But the longer he looked at the smiling faces all around him, the more unsettled he felt. Something about their superficial conversations and casual laughter rang hollow in his ears. A few of the International Prometheus Consortium board members were swapping stories about their extravagant vacations. The Sovereign was telling jokes and amusing personal anecdotes to a group of fawning admirers of his public media mogul persona. Few if any of the other guests were discussing anything of substance either.

These were individuals with uncommon insight into the state of the world and extraordinary accomplishments in their various fields. Some of them had remarkable skills and tremendous resources at their disposal. This was the only time each year when all of them were gathered together in one place for the singular purpose of showing their support for the betterment of humanity. Why, then, were they all indulging in trivial party banter when they could be discussing solutions to the climate crisis and other major problems facing humanity?

The front door swung wide open, interrupting the Preceptor's train of thought. He had mostly been ignoring the frequent opening and closing of the door, but this time the incoming guests caught his attention.

Sarah Athraigh had arrived.

"Sarah Athraigh!"

The Preceptor approached Sarah and her four companions with a broad smile. The newcomers stuck out like a sore thumb among the other guests who were all in formal or semiformal attire.

Sarah wore her usual no-nonsense street clothes: forest green shirt, black cargo pants, and black boots. Her friend with the healing abilities, Taelisin, could almost blend in with his light blue button-up shirt and navy blue cargo pants. The Anomalous Revolution militant, Patricia, definitely seemed out of place with her anime T-shirt, skirt full of bright clashing colors, and tablet computer strapped to a rainbow-colored armband on her right wrist.

The oddest of the lot, though, were the superhero and the musician. Hart wore his black latex superhero costume with the black utility belt and red hart logo on the chest. Jonny had a wispy, almost ethereal look, with elegantly gaunt features, short spiked hair, a loose-fitting silk shirt and silk bell bottoms, pointy shoes, and a translucent peacock blue-green electric guitar slung over his shoulder.

Together, the five of them brought a palpable Anomalous presence into the room. Heads were already turning before the Preceptor even crossed the short distance between them.

"Glad you could make it!" The Preceptor shook everyone's hand, starting with Sarah and finishing with Jonny. "You must be Jonny Glas! It's a pleasure to have a genuine rock star among us."

"Quite a fancy shindig you've got here." Jonny lifted a glass of wine from a passing server's tray and took a quick drink. "You're the one with the fancy secret base, then, and the golden crown and such?"

The Preceptor smiled warmly, lifting a finger to his lips

to shush Jonny playfully.

"Our little secret. Come, let me introduce you to a few of the other guests."

The Preceptor led the group into the dining room for some introductions.

After reading Dr. Aino's report on Sarah's role in the Favorable Anomalies scenario, the Preceptor had done some research of his own. He found several Order contacts who might be able to help Sarah and her companions with their response to the climate crisis. He introduced Taliesin to the founder of a spiritual healing school, Patricia to a scientist who was involved in a particle accelerator research program, Hart to the director of an academic non-profit that was studying Real Life Superheroes, and Jonny to one of his biggest fans who also happened to be a billionaire.

With any luck, these contacts would be able to improve the group's access to institutional resources and authority, thus improving their ability to respond to the climate crisis on that level. Since these contacts were friends of Order, they would also hopefully help to steer Sarah and her crew away from any activities or solutions that were too Anomalous.

As her companions split off to focus on side conversations, Sarah walked with the Preceptor toward the stairs to the second floor. Before they started up the steps, however, Sarah saw a familiar face out of the corner of her eye.

"Percy!"

Before the Preceptor could object, Sarah strode confidently toward Percival Sword, Sovereign of Order. The Sovereign stood at the center of one of the side lounges, dressed in a black silk blazer and surrounded by a dozen women and half a dozen men as he smiled broadly and told charming stories with a twinkle in his eye and smooth, sweeping gestures to punctuate key points.

"And I said, 'If being successful is wrong, I don't want to be right!'"

Everyone in the room laughed, even a few people who

appeared to be involved in side conversations. Before he could continue with his next story, however, Sarah made her way through the crowd and repeated his name.

"Percy! The infamous Percival Sword! Fancy meeting you here."

Percival smiled warmly at Sarah, casting a cold glance over her shoulder at the Preceptor before returning his attention to her.

"Why, if it isn't Little Miss Chicken Little! Have you had a chance to check out that news site I recommended?"

Everyone in the circle around the Sovereign chuckled. The Preceptor placed a hand on Sarah's shoulder in an effort to draw her away from the conversation. Sarah smirked, brushing away the Preceptor's restraining hand before continuing.

"Yes, actually. And don't worry, I'll let you return to your little fan club in a minute here. I just have one question."

"Oh?" The Sovereign smiled with genuine curiosity. As he looked at Sarah, his icy blue pupils contracted slightly. The Preceptor found something about that cold, calculating look deeply unsettling, setting off alarm bells in his head as the Sovereign spoke. "This should be entertaining. And I am ever the entertainer, so do tell."

Sarah glared at the Sovereign.

"We both know the truth about climate change, but you don't seem to know what's coming. Will all of your money and power protect you when climate disasters create social upheaval that tears apart the very fabric of reality as we know it?"

For a long moment, the Sovereign stared at Sarah in silence, the smile fading from his lips. Then, he clapped his hands together in front of his chest, smiling broadly and extending his clasped hands in her direction.

"Bravo, Chicken Little! You're the only one here who gives a more dramatic speech than I do. Bravo!"

The Sovereign started clapping, and everyone around him followed suit. Just as Sarah was about to reply, she heard the Preceptor's voice whispering in her ear.

"Not now."

The Preceptor started walking back toward the stairs and motioned for Sarah to follow. Something about the conflict between the Sovereign and Sarah was deeply unsettling -- and his Preceptor's intuition told him that there was an Anomalous component to their clash of wills that he didn't fully understand. He needed to separate the two of them immediately before the situation spiraled out of control.

Sarah looked back at the Sovereign for a moment, pointing a finger at him with an angry glare.

"This isn't over, Sword. Change is coming, and you're in the way."

She brushed aside the Preceptor and pushed through the crowd, marching out of the room and back to the foot of the stairs. After a few moments, the Preceptor caught up to her, leaning in close to speak to her in hushed tones.

"You're the life of the party."

"What can I say. I have a conscience."

"That you do."

Sarah sighed in exasperation. "You say you want to do something about climate change. Isn't dealing with people like him a good start? Can't you just—"

"Tread carefully, Sarah." He glanced in the Sovereign's direction. He didn't want to reveal the Sovereign's role in Order, but he needed to say something to dissuade Sarah from escalating the conflict any further. "Direct confrontation is not the answer here. PEN News is one of the most advanced social engineering tools on the planet. He has more power than you can imagine. Fighting him head-on will get you nowhere."

"How else can I fight him? PEN is one of the worst climate science deniers on the planet. They're single-handedly brainwashing millions of people into believing that climate change isn't even happening. Doesn't that have to change in order to prevent the world from burning all the fossil fuels and triggering a climate apocalypse? Somebody has to stop them."

"You're still thinking like a rabble-rousing peasant,

Sarah. Stop fighting the power and start being the power. Find your power and wield it like a queen. If you don't like the way that PEN is leading the people, lead them another way."

"Lead them another way? Like you do?" She crossed her arms and glared at the Preceptor. "I don't want to be a social engineer like you. I want to be an activist. I want to inspire people to make up their own minds and take their own actions to create a better world."

The Preceptor smiled broadly. "That, my dear, is the highest form of social engineering. Like the architect who captures the rays of the sun to heat and light a home, or the—"

Suddenly, Edward Jamison from the International Prometheus Consortium walked up and interrupted the Preceptor. He stood a little too close to the Preceptor and seemed to be actively ignoring Sarah.

"Truman!" Jamison's thin-lipped smile, slightly flushed face, and cold grey eyes spoke of a deep anger beneath the thin facade of polite greeting. "The rumors are true, then. You really are consorting with terrorists."

The Preceptor cringed, his head twisting and lips curling as he drew breath with an audible hiss.

"Miss Athraigh, this is Edward Richard Jamison, President of the Board of the International Prometheus Consortium. Mr. Jamison, this is—"

"I know damned well who this is, Truman. I also know that one of your little front groups deposited a large sum of money in her bank account just days after she disrupted a press conference in front of our world headquarters."

"Miss Athraigh is an outside consultant. Her methods are unconventional, but—"

Jamison interrupted the Preceptor by placing a firm hand on his shoulder. "Come now, Truman. Have you been spending so much time in that little hideaway of yours that you've forgotten how things work out here in the real world? I speak on behalf of several members of the board who are very concerned about public perception of the petroleum industry.

If these gentlemen knew exactly the sort of company you keep, they might not be so eager to fund your little social engineering operation."

The Preceptor decided he was not in the mood for Jamison's escalating threats to the economic foundations of Order. He nonchalantly drew a handgun out of a hidden holster and planted the cold steel muzzle in the middle of Jamison's forehead.

Jamison gasped, his eyes widening and jaw dropping. A hush fell over the entire room, including Sarah. The Preceptor stared at Jamison with a look of cold contempt, letting the silence linger for a long moment before speaking to Jamison in a calm but firm tone.

"You, sir, have forgotten how the real world works. I could end you right now and control your assets within two hours. You're a valuable asset, but like all assets, you are replaceable. Never forget that."

Jamison took several slow steps back, bowing slightly in deference to the Preceptor. The Preceptor slid his gun back into its holster, smiling broadly and sweeping his arms wide open in a welcoming gesture to everyone in the room.

"So glad you could all make it! Please, have another drink on the house!"

The Preceptor grabbed his half-full glass of wine and casually headed toward the stairs. After exchanging confused looks and shrugged shoulders, the guests gradually returned to their various conversations. He took a few steps up the stairs and heard Sarah following him.

"Do you always brandish weapons at your party guests?"

The Preceptor smiled broadly. "Only the rude ones."

He led Sarah down the hall at the top of the stairs and into the private room where he had recently spoken with Congresswoman O'Neill. As soon as the Preceptor and Sarah walked through the door, Dr. Aino, Dr. Bharati, and Dr. Bharati's three staff all quietly left the room to give the Preceptor, the congresswoman, and Sarah some privacy.

"Sarah, allow me to introduce you to another new friend of mine. Sarah Athraigh, this is Congresswoman Irene O'Neill. Congresswoman O'Neill, this is Sarah Athraigh."

Sarah smiled broadly. "It's a pleasure to meet you, Congresswoman O'Neill."

"Please, call me Irene." She stood and approached Sarah, shaking her hand with a firm grip. "It's a pleasure to meet you as well. Not many people have had the pleasure of telling off Percival Sword in front of his own news cameras!"

Sarah and Irene laughed. The Preceptor chuckled, wagging his finger at Sarah with a sly smile.

"Naughty, naughty."

Sarah smirked. "I would have kept going if someone hadn't shot me full of tranquilizers."

The Preceptor laughed. "Yes, you would have. Discretion is the better part of valor, Sarah. Remember that next time."

"And the best defense is a good offense."

"I like your attitude, Sarah." Irene smiled warmly. "I can see what he sees in you. You remind me of myself before I became a politician. Bright, assertive, uncompromising."

"I've always been a big fan of yours. I would've voted for you if you were in my state."

"Thank you."

"Great!" The Preceptor clasped his hands together with a broad smile. "As you may know, Irene here has mostly focused on peace and social justice issues. She does, however, have some climate change news that may interest you. I'll let you two get to it!"

Without another word, the Preceptor slipped out the door, closing it behind himself to leave Sarah and Irene alone together.

As the Preceptor headed back downstairs, he breathed a sigh of relief. Now that Sarah and her companions had all connected with their new contacts, he could collect his thoughts and do some networking with the other guests. Before he could decide who to talk to next, a thought occurred to him.

Something had felt off about the Sovereign's interaction with Sarah -- and the other guests, for that matter. It all seemed normal on the surface, but something about it triggered red flags from his Preceptor's intuition.

The guests laughing at the Sovereign's jokes, even when they weren't really paying attention. The cold stare that seemed to be quietly but firmly probing Sarah for information. The lingering sense that having Sarah and the Sovereign in the same room together was dangerous, above and beyond the obvious potential for verbal or physical confrontation.

And it wasn't just coming from Sarah. Was there something Anomalous about the Sovereign too?

The Preceptor pulled out his tablet and opened a new message to Dr. Aino.

Recalculate Percival Sword's Verwechseln score. Review his profile for any Anomalous activity, especially signs of any Anomalous social or mental abilities that may have gone unnoticed. Keep this discreet and send the results directly to me.

After the Preceptor sent his message, he noticed a crowd gathering in the dining room. Jonny, Taliesin, and Hart were singing a simple song together. Patricia was dancing with what appeared to be a small robotic garden gnome. The gnome was standing on the dining room table and swaying back and forth awkwardly to the music. Jonny was playing his guitar, filling the room with the sound of a lute as the three men and a growing number of audience members sang along to a lively drinking tune.

> *"Oh, I've drank me some whiskey and wine and ale*
> *But never a drop from beneath the shale*
> *The glaciers would melt and the sea would boil*
> *If I drank me a drop of your dirty oil."*

The three men sang half a dozen verses, coming back to the same refrain over and over again. The serving staff struggled to make their way through the crowd as everyone near the dining room took up glasses of wine, shots of whiskey, and bottles of craft beers, some of them singing along to the refrain or clapping along to the beat. A group of about a dozen men, including the Sovereign and Jamison, glared in their general direction and stormed upstairs or walked out the front door.

The Preceptor noticed Sarah watching the performance from the foot of the stairs. When she stepped forward and joined the chorus, the gathered guests grew even more enthusiastic in their support, clapping and cheering while several people pulled out their cell phones and started recording. When they were done singing, the crowd applauded heartily.

The Preceptor made his way to the front of the crowd, clapping along with the guests for a few moments before sweeping his hands dramatically to present Jonny to his audience.

"Let's hear it again for Jonny Glas!" As the audience applauded, the Preceptor stepped forward and gave Jonny's shoulder a few hard pats. "Hope you and your friends have a good trip home, Jonny. In the meantime, everyone else can join me in the pavilion out back for the evening's main performance!"

As the Preceptor led the crowd out the back door, Jonny cast Sarah a quizzical look.

"Home? Are we leaving, love?"

Sarah smirked. "That's his way of saying that we should go before he makes us go."

"Aww!" Patricia pouted, picking up her robotic gnome and cradling him in one of her arms like a small child. "Is this because those oil men didn't like our song? Boo hoo." With her free hand, she drank a shot of whiskey, slamming the empty shot glass on the table with an impish grin. "If they don't like our songs, make them go!"

The Preceptor ignored Sarah and her companions as he continued leading the other guests out to the large wooden pavilion behind the main building. Once the majority of the guests had moved to the pavilion, he stepped back inside.

The ground floor of the main building was now mostly empty aside from several servers in white tuxedos and an elderly couple who were quietly discussing their plans for the rest of the evening. The Preceptor found his glass of wine and finished it with several quick gulps. He pulled out his tablet, requested transport back to the Panopticon, and leaned against the nearest wall with a sigh.

CHAPTER 15

The Preceptor sat alone in the conference room, reviewing the latest daily updates from his staff on his tablet.

For the first time in recent memory, the top items on the list had nothing to do with climate change, or at least nothing obvious. A recent wave of cyberattacks on all of the world's major intelligence communities had been linked to a single Anomalous operative somewhere in South Korea, and a botched false flag operation in the Middle East had required direct Order intervention to prevent a major escalation in tensions between nuclear powers.

Of course, the Preceptor's eye was still drawn to the climate-related items lower on the list. Order's internal projections of the consequences of catastrophic climate change had once again been revised to indicate a more dire outlook for the coming decades. Sea level rise, major hurricanes, floods, droughts, heat waves, and wildfires were all going to be more damaging than initially projected due to new research about feedback loops as well as the ongoing failure of world governments to accelerate global emissions reduction. A new analysis also indicated that the economic and political consequences of recent and near-term warming were worse than initially projected.

None of this was entirely new or surprising information. It was, in fact, what he expected to read at this point. But that didn't make it any more encouraging.

The conference room door slid open. Dr. Aino stepped through and bowed slightly to the Preceptor, pausing near the doorway.

"Buongiorno, Preceptor."

The Preceptor rose to his feet and returned the bow.

"Good day to you too, Toshi. Please, have a seat."

The two men took their seats, with the Preceptor sitting at the head of the table and Dr. Aino sitting next to him. The Preceptor noticed that Dr. Aino's voice and manner seemed very subdued.

"Is something wrong, Toshi? Is it related to my request?"

"Yes, Preceptor. And... yes."

Dr. Aino pulled a small pink tablet computer out of his inner coat pocket. It had a cracked screen that appeared to be dead. When he swiped the screen in a certain pattern, though, it came back to life, and he entered a numerical code..

"I've brought the updated file to you on a secure device. We must not update it in the official Order records, you see. We must be very careful in case..." He cleared his throat anxiously. "Choose a new lock pattern and code for the device, Preceptor, and it will be for your eyes only. The device has no wireless connectivity and will stop working if anyone tampers with it."

The Preceptor nodded, taking the device and entering his own new lock pattern and code. The screen went blank, seemingly dead. He entered the pattern and code again and it sprang back to life. This time, it displayed the Sovereign's updated Verwechseln scale report. The top of the page included a one-line summary in large print.

Percival Sword. Verwechseln: 8.4. (Confidence: High. Range: 5.9 to 8.8.)

The Preceptor's pulse quickened. 8.4 was an incredibly high Verwechseln score for an individual human being. There were a handful of groups like Anomalous Revolution that made it into the 7 or 8 range due to their unbridled fanaticism and significant power to affect change. To earn such a high score, an individual would have to be capable of single-handedly threatening the very existence of Order itself.

The Preceptor started reading the full report. After a few moments, he remembered that Dr. Aino was still in the room.

He set the report aside for the moment, returning his attention to Dr. Aino.

"My suspicions were correct, then?"

"Yes, Preceptor. I am not a specialist in this field, of course. The Insight maintains all official Verwechseln reports. But I am familiar with many methodologies of analyzing Anomalous threats due to my work with the metamodel and the scenarios. This includes the Verwechseln scoring system."

"Of course. What did you find out?"

"The exact details are uncertain, I'm afraid. This is why there is a wide range in the full set of scores. But the presence of Anomalous activity is undeniable." He leaned in closer, lowering his voice to a whisper. "I have analyzed his public and private data carefully. He has a long history of persuading people to do what he wants."

The Preceptor lowered his voice to match Dr. Aino's whisper.

"Yes, but that's nothing out of the ordinary, is it? He's a self-made billionaire. He's known for his charisma and--"

Dr. Aino shook his head, waving his hands dismissively.

"This is no ordinary situation, Preceptor. Some of these are people who made statements against him and his projects, but changed their mind after meeting him in person. Some were strangers or even powerful rivals who suddenly offered him gifts or concessions after a single meeting. Some rivals may have revealed company secrets to him. Some of these people even expressed regret or confusion about their own behavior afterward. They did not do these things willingly, you see. But they did them. Any one incident seems almost harmless. Coincidental, perhaps. But the long-term pattern is clear."

"Which means--"

"Which means, my friend, he has some way of making people do things against their will. Maybe he has a preternatural gift for the art of persuasion. Maybe he has a way of quietly blackmailing people without being detected. Or maybe..." He put one hand on the side of his head and pointed his other hand at the Preceptor's head. "Telepathy. Aggressive telepathy. Changing the thoughts and behaviors of others at will."

The Preceptor leaned back in his chair and sighed. He felt a flood of intuition confirming what Dr. Aino was describing. Percival Sword had an innate ability to read people's minds and push them to do things against their will.

Minor forms of empathy and telepathy were surprisingly common, but anything this powerful was exceedingly rare -- and inherently dangerous. This meant that Sovereign of Order was now one of the most Anomalous individuals known to Order.

The Preceptor read more of the report, then looked back up at Dr. Aino.

"How did we miss this?"

"That is unclear, Preceptor. The Council of Order did review his record and Verwechseln score before appointing him Sovereign of Order. They came to a much different conclusion at that time. Maybe they had less information at the time than we do now. Or maybe they were careless because he was already a trusted figure, a member of the Council. Or maybe..."

"Or maybe he used his Anomalous abilities to persuade them that he wasn't an Anomalous threat."

"Precisely. In any case, there is one bit of good news, perhaps."

"Good. I could use some good news. What is it?"

"There may be limits to this ability. It only seems to happen after a face-to-face meeting. People who have never met him face-to-face seem much more likely to reject his influence. And some people may be resistant or immune. Perhaps Sarah Athraigh, for example. Perhaps even you, Preceptor, since you are able to ask these questions, when no one else in Order has."

"Hmm." After a few moments of thought, the Preceptor's eyes lit up. "It's the Egregore. My connection to the Egregore of Order protects me."

"Ah, yes, the Egregore. The group mind of Order."

"Yes."

"I hope you are right, Preceptor." Dr. Aino paused. "I am more of a computer person. The esoteric arts as such are not my forte, you see. What little I know of the Egregore is what I have read in books as a student and analyst. But I hope that whatever has protected you so far, continues protecting you. For your sake, and for all of our sakes."

"Yes. Here's hoping."

Cerulean waves crashed against the black sands of the rocky shoreline, transforming the edge of the water into white foam and mist for a few seconds before sliding back into the ocean. The sky overhead was a wide expanse of crystal blue broken only by the jagged black cliffs to the east and a distant storm approaching from over the ocean to the west. The only evidence of human habitation anywhere in sight was a small single-storey building with three glass walls facing the ocean and a fourth white marble wall with its back to the cliffs.

The Preceptor and the Insight walked together along the shore. The air was filled with the strong scent of saltwater and wet sand. The Preceptor was wearing his usual white button-up shirt and cargo pants with the addition of a black wool coat to guard against the chill in the air. The Insight was wearing a neon blue blouse, black slacks, and a black overcoat that rustled in the wind coming in from the ocean. Her long flame-red hair was drawn back into a tight braid that stood out against the dark fabric of her coat and the beach's many shades of blue, grey, and black.

For several minutes, they walked together in silence, looking out at the waves, up at the cliffs, and down at the black sand, which was actually composed of shiny black pebbles of various sizes. Eventually, the Preceptor spoke.

"So this is where we've been having our meetings."

The Insight laughed. "Yes. Do you like it?"

"Yes."

They walked a little farther down the beach, venturing just out of sight of the small marble building that had served as the model for the Insight's favorite teleconference room theme. Once they were alone, the Preceptor stopped on the edge of the water, staring out at the ocean.

"Do you know why I asked you to meet me here?"

"I assumed it was because you missed me."

The Preceptor smiled. "I do. But that's not the only reason."

The Insight returned the smile. "Yes. I know you too well to assume that any personal sentiment was the only reason, or even the main reason. But I'm sure it was a factor. You could have chosen almost any secluded location in the world, but you chose here. A place that you knew I cherished."

"Yes. Plans within plans."

The Preceptor hesitated. He had rehearsed the next part of the conversation dozens of times on the flight to Iceland, but it never seemed to go the way he wanted it to in his head. There was no turning back now, though, so he decided to go with the simple and direct approach.

"I need to know if you're with me on the Favorable Anomalies scenario."

"With you?" The Insight glanced over at him, then looked out toward the ocean. "I believe in evidence-based policy. And the evidence indicates that Favorable Anomalies has the highest likelihood of a favorable outcome for Order and the world generally."

The Preceptor nodded. "And what about the Sovereign's directive? This idea that we must consider it a successful outcome to let seven billion die while a few hundred million carry on the work of Order?"

The Insight stared out at the ocean. At first, the Preceptor wondered if she was going to respond at all. Eventually, she spoke.

"The Sovereign has spoken. We have to consider it as a possibility. But that doesn't mean we should just let it become a reality. We should try to find another way."

"Exactly. My thoughts exactly."

The Preceptor placed a hand on the Insight's shoulder. Something in her brilliant blue eyes softened in response to his light-handed touch.

"Kendra. Please, whatever you do, don't meet with the Sovereign for any reason."

A look of confusion flashed across her face.

"Is it that bad?"

"Worse. It's not just about his depopulation directive anymore. He's a direct threat to Order. Personally."

The Preceptor reached into his coat pocket, pulling out the broken tablet that Dr. Aino had given him. After entering his unlock pattern and code, he placed the device in her hands.

"Enter your own pattern and code and read this."

The Insight took the broken tablet, entered her pattern and code, and started reading. The two of them stood together in silence for several minutes while she studied the details of Percival Sword's entire updated Verwechseln report. Her eyes widened at the beginning, but as she continued reading, she eventually she settled into a state of calm concentration.

When she was done, she offered to return the device to the Preceptor, but he refused it with a wave of his hand.

"Keep it. You're the Insight. You should have the most accurate version of the Sovereign of Order's Verwechseln report. But we can't risk updating his official profile with this new information. And if anything happens to me--"

She placed a hand on his shoulder.

"Don't talk like that, Truman. If this is all true, it's very serious. But we'll get through it. Order will get through it."

"Yes. But I have to prepare for every eventuality. If anything happens to me, and you think he's involved, expose him. I can't move against him now because he has too much support. The Council agrees with his depopulation directive, and I'm confident the Catalyst and Guardian are with him on that too. If I expose him now, he'll spin it as a power play on my part. But if he moves against me, or does anything else that places his own interests above the interests of Order, that might be enough to change their minds."

The Insight paused, looking out across the ocean as she considered his words.

"What about decrowning? Concealing this Anomalous ability would be sufficient grounds. There is precedent."

The Preceptor sighed. "Yes, but not much. Only one Sovereign has ever been involuntarily decrowned by the Council. Unless you count the handful of others in centuries past who were probably 'retired' prematurely. There's also the fact that his Anomalous abilities would allow him to interfere with the process. We would have to detain him and keep him away from the Council while they deliberated -- which is impossible as long as he has the Guardian on his side."

"So what do we do?"

"We watch and wait for him to make a mistake. Discreetly look for an opportunity to expose his Anomalous ability and any use of it against fellow Initiates. Create such an opportunity, if possible."

"And in the meantime, obey his every directive."

"Yes. For the time being, he is still Sovereign of Order. The moment we openly disobey him, we'd better be prepared to expose him. Otherwise, we're the ones who will be found in defiance of Order."

A long silence lingered between them, broken only by the sound of the waves crashing on the sand and the foam lapping at their boots. The storm that the Preceptor had noticed approaching earlier was already almost upon them, darkening the sky with thick grey clouds. The winds picked up, lending an extra sharpness to the damp chill in the air.

The Preceptor turned away from the Insight and the ocean, walking back toward the small marble and glass building down the beach from where they were standing. The Insight soon followed, catching up and walking by his side as they approached the building.

There were still some details to discuss -- how to communicate at a distance without being intercepted by the Sovereign, and how to respond to his various likely next moves. But the most important question was now settled.

He wasn't in this alone. She was with him.

CHAPTER 16

The Preceptor sat at his cobalt blue desk in the Panopticon, reviewing the latest surveillance report on Sarah Athraigh.

Sarah and her companions had apparently just organized an unpermitted free concert and march in New York to promote their latest round of green initiatives. Jonny Glas was using his fame and broad fan base to draw attention to the cause through new climate-themed music and public performances. Congresswoman O'Neill was working on a comprehensive climate mitigation and adaptation bill that would have considerable impact if it could somehow make it out of committee and get enough votes to pass. Together, they were making tangible, quantifiable progress toward their goal of cultural and institutional shifts around fossil fuels and climate change.

And yet, it still wasn't enough. It was more than Order had been achieving without them, and it was projected to grow very quickly into a major global movement for climate action. But it still wasn't enough to avert a complete global crash sometime in the 2050s. Some as-yet undiscovered Anomalous element was still required to prevent the whole system from crashing during the decades it would take for these ideas and proposals to become manifest realities.

The Preceptor left his desk and walked over to the large crystal globe at the center of the Panopticon. He used his tablet to pull up the Standard scenario and set it to display on the Eye for one hundred cycles. The various shades of green, yellow, orange, and red all bled together into a single unbroken sea of crimson that quickly faded to black. Each repetition was the same -- a world full of color and life bleeding out and fading into oblivion.

After watching a few dozen repetitions, the Preceptor walked away from the pulsing globe and headed to the elevator.

The Preceptor's nearly silent black helicopter touched down on the simple concrete helipad near the center of the complex. After the three Initiates in his primary security detail took a few moments to look around for any unexpected threats, the Preceptor emerged from the helicopter and examined his surroundings.

The Sonnenberg Solar Sanctuary was a sprawling industrial complex located in a large grassy clearing in the middle of the woods in central Colorado. The helicopter pad was surrounded by several large log cabins and over a dozen green sheet metal buildings of various shapes and sizes. Every building had solar panels, solar water heaters, or both on the roof, with a large field to the south filled with numerous rows of solar panels on metal racks. The entire complex was surrounded by thick forest cover, with lodgepole pines and other evergreens rising all around the buildings and fields of panels. The snow-capped peaks of Mount Elbert and its neighbors loomed large beyond the treetops, anchoring the entire landscape and their place in it.

When the Preceptor stepped out of the helicopter, there was still no one there to greet him. While he was admiring the view, a middle-aged woman in a crisp kelly green pantsuit emerged from the nearest log cabin at a brisk walk, followed closely by a younger man and woman who both wore black slacks and neon green polo shirts. The woman leading the small group approached the Preceptor and gave him a firm handshake.

"Welcome, Dr. Stuart! I'm Tiffany Sonnenberg. Welcome to Sonnenberg Solar Sanctuary!"

"Thank you, Ms. Sonnenberg."

"Please, call me Tiffany. And I apologize for the delay.

We were expecting you, but we didn't hear your helicopter. You really do have silent helicopters, don't you?" She laughed. "Please, allow me to give you the tour."

Tiffany and her two assistants led the Preceptor and his security detail down several of the roads that connected the various buildings of the complex. As they walked by each building, she explained its purpose, taking a peek inside a few of them to offer the Preceptor a glimpse of the site's operations. Her assistants chimed in occasionally to provide additional details. There were almost a dozen large two-storey and three-storey log cabins being used as offices, meeting spaces, and shared living quarters. Several of the smaller sheet metal buildings were home to a machine shop, maker space, and storage areas. The largest building was a photovoltaic panel manufacturing center that was two storeys tall and larger than a football field.

The Preceptor listened and nodded occasionally, taking a few notes on his tablet as they walked. At the end of the tour, Tiffany pointed to the cabin that she had come out of when the Preceptor arrived.

"Now that the tour is taken care of, I believe we have some business to attend to. Would you care to join me in my office?"

"Yes."

"Alright." Tiffany turned to her two assistants. "Miranda, Stefan, why don't you take an early lunch? I'll see you at our one o'clock meeting."

Miranda and Stefan bowed slightly, then headed down the road. Tiffany led the Preceptor to her office.

The interior of the cabin was much more elegantly decorated than the simple wood exterior. Bright full-spectrum LED lights illuminated the smooth white walls and finished hardwood floor of the spacious lobby. Dozens of green potted plants were complemented by a green marble front desk, several green leather chairs, and a round glass table with a slight green tint. Plentiful natural light poured in through large south-facing picture windows and solar tubes embedded in the ceiling even though it was a mostly-cloudy day. The young woman behind the front desk waved to Tiffany and the Preceptor with a smile as Tiffany opened a big wood door and stepped inside.

Tiffany's office was decorated with a similar aesthetic to the lobby -- white walls, potted plants, framed photos and technical schematics of solar panels, and a big wooden desk that was spotless except for a slightly overflowing inbox. She sat behind the desk and offered the Preceptor the seat across from her. When they were both seated, she was the first to speak.

"So. Tell me more about this... opportunity."

"Yes." The Preceptor paused. "How much do you already know?"

"Not much." Tiffany laughed. "The way Irene describes it, you sound like the Men in Black. Is that an apt comparison?"

The Preceptor smiled.

"A colorful analogy. We operate with a degree of discretion, but there's nothing sinister about what we do. Think of us as a global thinktank whose primary mission is to facilitate the evolution of human consciousness and advancement of human progress."

"So... a global thinktank with a private army."

The Preceptor smirked, dismissing the comment with a wave of his hand.

"We don't have a private army. Armies are organized by governments." The smile vanished from the Preceptor's lips. He leaned forward slightly, looking Tiffany straight in the eye. "We organize governments. Every government in the world is in some way involved in our efforts -- and we are involved in theirs. This sometimes requires the judicious application of direct interventions -- but mostly it involves rigorous observation, analysis, and light-handed social engineering at the macro and micro scales. Most of what we do isn't quite as exciting as the romanticized version of our work circulating in urban legends. But we get the job done."

Tiffany nodded, mulling over his words.

"So you don't go around disappearing people?"

"Not unless they're far more dangerous than the dissidents your government is already disappearing."

Tiffany's eyes widened. She cleared her throat, pausing a moment to gather her thoughts.

"Fair enough. Tell me then, where do I fit in? Irene said you're looking for allies in the renewable energy industry. But we're really not the Men in Black type, if you'll forgive the colorful analogy. We tend to be independent thinkers. A few steps outside of the norm. Visionaries chasing dreams of a clean energy future. Some of us are even preppers who fear the sort of global government you seem to be describing."

"Which is why we haven't had much direct contact with your industry leaders until now. But times have changed. The industry is growing fast enough to alter the balance of the global economy. You're becoming major players -- and you're going mainstream. Many of your customers and investors value renewables primarily for their economic benefits. My organization can help you to deliver those benefits -- and eventually render the entire fossil fuel industry obsolete."

"Oh, the fossil fuel industry's already obsolete. They just haven't gotten the memo yet."

Tiffany laughed loudly at her own joke. The Preceptor smiled and nodded.

"Yes, they're on their way out. But they're not there yet. They still have tremendous power, economically and politically. They have no intention of surrendering that power anytime soon. But I'm increasingly of the opinion that we need to take extraordinary action to accelerate the transition to cleaner energy sources."

"Good. I have to ask, though." Tiffany paused, looking off into the distance thoughtfully for a moment before continuing. "Aren't you in bed with the fossil fuel industry? I mean, the U.S. government, and so many other governments, seem to--"

"Traditionally, yes. They've been our allies since the dawn of the industrial age. But the climate--"

Tiffany blinked in surprise.

"Wait a minute. Dawn of the industrial age. You've been around that long?"

"Yes. Longer. But the climate crisis requires us to shift away from fossil fuels as rapidly as possible without causing global collapse."

"Global collapse. You mean climate apocalypse?"

"We avoid theologically tinged language when possible. But yes, some would call it a climate apocalypse. The end of the modern world as we know it. Transition too slowly and catastrophic climate change wreaks havoc on global society. Transition too quickly and global society breaks down. Either error leads to disastrous outcomes. Economies collapse; wars break out; fossil fuel oligarchs hold onto their last vestiges of power with unchecked violence and corruption of local governments. It's very difficult to project the exact outcome, but very easy to determine that it will not result in any semblance of a decent, modern human society. There will be mass suffering and death on a global scale unless we do something to stop it."

Tiffany leaned back in her chair and sighed. She sat there for a moment, lost in thought. Eventually, she leaned forward and spoke.

"So, hypothetically speaking, what do I do?"

The Preceptor smiled. "It's very simple. You and your company donate no less than ten percent of your profits to us. Some of that will go directly to our foundation. Some will go to political campaigns, nonprofits, or other allied entities. In return, we favor your company and use the majority of your funds to accelerate the transition away from fossil fuels."

Tiffany looked at the Preceptor somewhat skeptically.

"Favor? What does that mean?"

"It means new contracts suddenly coming your way. Government contracts, private contracts. We put the word out to our network that you're the go-to supplier for photovoltaic modules and any other goods and services you're selling. Most of the people that we send your way won't even know that we had a hand in it. You'll just see a sudden increase in business."

"And then when we make more profit, we'll have more money to send your way."

The Preceptor smiled broadly. "Yes. You get more profits, we get more funding, and the transition to clean energy accelerates. Everyone's a winner."

Tiffany laughed.

"Yes, that makes sense. But what about the fossil fuel industry? How much do they donate to you? I hate to keep coming back to that, but surely you can understand my concern here. They must be giving you more money than all of the renewable energy industries combined can possibly --"

"It's not just about the money. We do need money to operate, but far less than you might imagine due to our extensive influence over other people's money. And no amount of money can purchase our favor if the donor's intentions stand in conflict with our mission. The intention of the fossil fuels industry to maintain its global empire indefinitely is increasingly coming into conflict with our mission. So one penny of steady renewable money is worth a thousand dollars of oil, gas, or coal money -- especially since you're on the rise and they're on the decline. Your donation may be tiny now, but in twenty years, it will be substantial. We look forward to helping make that happen sooner rather than later. If, of course, you're willing to work with us."

Tiffany leaned back in her big leather executive chair, tapping her fingers together, lost in thought. She stared off into the distance for a few moments before replying.

"Ten percent of our profits is a lot to ask when I have little to go on but your word and a referral from a friend."

The Preceptor brushed aside her concerns with a wave of his hand.

"When your profits jump by twenty or thirty percent in the first year, you'll hardly even notice the donation anymore. Besides, most of it will be tax deductible. You'll be saving on taxes, securing new clients, and putting another nail in the coffin of your fossil fuels competitors, all in one fell swoop."

Tiffany laughed. "You should be in sales. When you put it that way, it's hard to resist. Do you have any paperwork for me to review, or--"

"No paperwork. Just a handshake and a routing number. Make a transfer once per quarter and you'll meet with me or my staff once per quarter to discuss our progress or answer any questions."

"And I can change my mind at any time?"

"Yes."

"No one will come and disappear me if I change my mind and stop making payments?"

The Preceptor smiled. "No. There are no refunds, of course, but you can stop at any time."

"Sounds good, then. You have yourself a deal."

Tiffany stood up and walked around to the front of her desk. The Preceptor rose to his feet and shook her hand.

CHAPTER 17

The great stone pillars and walls of the Gateway of India rose above the cobblestone promenade looking out over the Arabian Sea. It wasn't a particularly tall monument, with the larger central stone arch measuring only eight-five feet high. But the regal rising of the arches, four crowning turrets, and uncommon integration of Hindu and Muslim architectural styles granted it an air of power and majesty, as did its prominence on the shores of the bay.

The Preceptor and the Catalyst walked side by side along the promenade, keeping close to one another so that their conversation would easily be lost amidst the hustle and bustle of the many tourists and locals visiting the renowned landmark on any given day. Both men were wearing their usual business casual street clothes -- the Preceptor in a white button-up shirt and the Catalyst in a green button-up shirt, with both men wearing similar black cargo pants. They would have easily blended in with the tourists if it weren't for the fact that they each had a separate contingent of a dozen Initiates of Order in black suits and dark sunglasses shadowing them as they strolled along the promenade and plaza at the foot of the monument.

"Welcome to Mumbai, Preceptor. Is this your first time here?"

"No, but it's been a while. It's a bit hotter than Colorado this time of year."

The Catalyst laughed, wiping a few beads of sweat from his brow.

"Yes, I'm sure it is. Honestly, I've considered moving my office to a cooler climate. But relocating the entire operation wouldn't be cheap, and we have such a good network here. There's a lot happening in this city, after all. And I spend most of my time indoors anyway. I could be anywhere in the world, really. So tell me, what brings you to Mumbai? Business or pleasure?"

"Business, I'm afraid. I have a few other stops in the region, but I mostly came here to meet with you in person."

"Oh?" The Catalyst glanced at the Preceptor curiously. "Telepresence getting a bit too impersonal for you? I've always been a big fan, but it's not for everyone."

"Something like that." The Preceptor paused. "Tell me, how's that campaign we talked about coming along? The fossil fuels intervention? I haven't heard much from you about it."

The Catalyst's eyes widened slightly. He looked away from the Preceptor, staring out over the bay.

"Oh, you know how it goes with social engineering campaigns. Research, analysis, figuring out how to quantify the results and act on them strategically. There's been a slight uptick in negative perceptions of the industry, but it's too soon to tell if it's due to our efforts or other factors."

"And the backup plan for a decapitation attack on the fossil fuel industry?"

The Catalyst stopped in place, looking around nervously and lowering his voice to a whisper.

"Do you really want to talk about that in a public place, Truman? Didn't the Sovereign--"

"The Sovereign said that a decap attack against the fossil fuel industry goes against Order policy. I say that we need to be prepared for all reasonable contingencies, even those that aren't currently in alignment with Order policy. Just because it's not the favored option doesn't mean that we shouldn't prepare for it. If something happens that changes the Council's mind on the subject, we need to be ready to act immediately."

"Well, I..." The Catalyst cleared his throat, anxiously scanning his surroundings. "I've been trying not to get in the middle of this... disagreement you have with the Sovereign. I do have a broad strokes outline of how a decap attack would go down, but nothing actionable yet."

"Make it actionable."

"I--"

The Preceptor put a hand on the Catalyst's shoulder.

"Make. It. Actionable."

The Preceptor let go of the Catalyst's shoulder and started walking. The Catalyst followed him, quickening his pace in order to catch up. Once they were walking side by side again, the Preceptor continued.

"Keep it off the books if you have to. Blame it on me if you have to. But I want to know that we can move on this at a moment's notice if necessary. I'm not talking about violating chain of command here -- I would only act on this with the Council's approval. But we need to be ready to act when the time comes. Have I made myself clear?"

"Yes, Preceptor."

"Good."

The Preceptor sat in the telepresence room across from the Insight. The room was set to use her custom Iceland theme. The floor and wall to his left were made of white marble with gold veins, partially obscured by a long and tall bookcase. The other walls and ceiling were made of glass, revealing the expansive black sand beach where they had walked together at their last meeting.

Before the Insight even spoke, the Preceptor knew that something was off. She had a world-weary look about her, with a hint of tiredness in her eyes, her hair drawn back in a simple ponytail rather than the usual braid, and her usual elegant color-coordinated outfit replaced with a simple black blouse and black cargo pants.

"Good morning, Insight."

"Good morning, Preceptor." A slight smile brightened

her face. "I see you've taken a fancy to my Iceland theme."

"Yes. I wish we were still there in person."

"I do too."

There was a moment of silence between them. Eventually, the Preceptor spoke.

"Do you have any news about the problem we discussed?"

"Not much aside from further confirmation of what we already suspected. I'd love to do some more thorough surveillance, but it won't be easy to do that without his knowledge. I'm working on it. In the meantime, we have a serious problem in the other direction."

The Insight picked up her tablet and used it to display a file on the wall between them. A rectangular slab of white marble appeared in the air above the conference table, hovering in place and displaying the contents of the file in finely chiseled black lettering.

Eutopia Engine: Strategic Analysis.

The Preceptor's pulse quickened as his intuition rang out like an alarm bell. Whatever this was, it was associated with Sarah Athraigh -- and might be a game-changer for the Favorable Anomalies scenario.

He started reading the document, then noticed that it was a long and complex report filled with charts, graphs, tables, and commentary on various metamodel scenarios. Rather than reading the full document while the Insight waited, he nudged the large marble display aside and looked back up at her.

"What do we have here?"

"It's an AR project called the Eutopia Engine. Based on the timing and a few other details, we think that Sarah Athraigh's people may be involved."

"Yes, this is definitely her work, or her people's work."

"I'm sorry to hear that. I'm recommending that we shut it down."

"Really?"

"Yes. Take a look at the executive summary."

The Preceptor pulled up the report, scrolled back to the

beginning, and read the one-page summary. It described the Eutopia Engine as an "engine for social change" -- a new online social network and task management system that allowed its users to post action proposals, list resources they had available, and communicate with each other about vision and strategy for transforming their local communities and societies for the better. The system analyzed the data and suggested connections between the users, projects, and resources. The summary concluded somewhat abruptly by asserting that this network posed an existential threat to Order and must be influenced or neutralized.

When the Preceptor was done reading, he pushed the report aside again so that he could get a clear view of the Insight while they spoke.

"I see. What seems to be the problem? How is this Anomalous enough to pose an existential threat to Order? It sounds harmless enough so far."

"There are several problems. The two most pressing ones are the technology and the projects. The network can be accessed using everyday hardware and software, but the server or servers that power it are definitely Anomalous. We can't even verify where they are or what operating systems they're running, much less how they work or how to gain access. And some of the projects the alpha testers are posting are harmless, like raising money to feed the hungry or install solar panels. But several of the projects and user profiles reference awareness of Order and express anti-Order goals."

"I see."

The Preceptor skimmed the rest of the report, paying special attention to the summaries and graphs related to explicit anti-Order content. He also opened a web browser on his tablet and perused the Eutopia Engine website. All of the basic project and user profile information was readily available to anyone who wasn't even signed in with a free account. Most of it did seem harmless, and probably beneficial to the Favorable Anomalies scenario given the emphasis on climate-related projects. But seeing prominent anti-Order discourse on a public website was disconcerting. Anomalous Revolution had plenty of anti-Order content online, but it was all on the dark web. Any Order-related content on the clearnet was usually taken down by Order operatives within hours, with the poster assigned to monitoring or neutralization.

"Yes. This is a problem." The Preceptor paused, tapping his fingers on the desk in front of him. "And you can't locate these servers? How is that possible? I thought we could locate any device connected to the internet."

"They seem to use some sort of relay system. All of the traffic is routed through a handful of simple relays that communicate wirelessly with the servers in some Anomalous way that we don't fully understand. Two of our field operatives had physical access to one of these relays for over an hour and couldn't even begin to figure out how it works. We think the relay itself was built with off-the-shelf tech, but whatever server it communicates with has to be Anomalous. The server seems to be transmitting data to and from these relays without the use of any network hardware or software, which makes no sense by normal computing standards."

"Hmm." The Preceptor stared off into space, lost in thought. "Share everything you've got with Dr. Aino. If anyone can figure this out, it's him. In the meantime, we're going to have to monitor and influence this thing using the public website. Anyone can create a basic user account, right?"

"Yes."

"Then we'll create some dummy accounts and use them to gather more data. Maybe we can even shift the tone of this thing in a better direction. Convince other users that the emphasis should be on tangible climate action, not chasing after some secret society that may or may not exist. The usual deflect and distract approach."

The Insight nodded. "Do you want me to contact the Catalyst? That seems like the sort of social engineering project that he and his team specialize in."

"No. I'll take care of it. I've got a few people who should be up to the task. Thank you for the report. I look forward to reading it in full when I'm back at my desk."

The Insight smiled slightly. "I do what I can."

"You do excellent work. Thank you. For the Victory of Order."

"For the Victory of Order."

The Preceptor tapped on his tablet, closing the connection to the Insight. The convincing illusion of the meeting space in Iceland faded to white, leaving the Preceptor sitting alone in a ten-foot cube room with smooth, bright white walls. He sighed, staring at the blank wall in front of him for several seconds before rising to his feet and heading out of the conference room.

CHAPTER 18

The Preceptor sat at his desk in the Panopticon, reviewing the Insight's full report on the Eutopia Engine.

On the bright side, the potential for Eutopia to accelerate the transition toward a zero emissions energy infrastructure was almost limitless. The project was still in alpha testing, but if it achieved its stated goals, it would soon mobilize millions of people in a very organic and effective way toward the completion of increasingly numerous and sophisticated community projects, many of them with a climate-related component. Emissions would start to diminish significantly without any intervention whatsoever from centralized institutions, and those institutions would likely shift course to catch up with changing realities on the ground. This quirky activist project might actually play a pivotal role in the successful realization of the Favorable Anomalies scenario.

On the dark side, the potential for Eutopia to wreak havoc on the world and the work of Order was equally limitless. There was no central leadership for Order to influence, and no central IT infrastructure for Order to tap into. Anomalous individuals, organizations, and perspectives could easily shift Eutopia in a radical populist direction, encouraging growing dissent against governments and Order itself. There were already a handful of projects that specifically targeted Order and its operations in some tangible way, and there was nothing stopping the creation of more such projects. There wasn't much they could do about it without conducting sweeping raids to confiscate all of the Eutopia relays currently in operation -- and that would become harder the longer they waited.

The Preceptor sighed. He closed the Eutopia Engine report and opened up a video chat with Dr. Aino.

"Good morning, Toshi."

"Buongiorno, Preceptor! Are you calling about the Eutopia Engine?"

The Preceptor smiled. "Yes, Toshi. Have you had a chance to look over the report and the data from the Insight?"

"I have, Preceptor! To me, this is very exciting news. I see the potential threat, of course. But the technology is fascinating, and the potential good it may do is considerable, if used responsibly."

"Agreed. What can you tell me about the technology?"

"Not much, Preceptor. The relays are very simple, you see, but the servers must be quite Anomalous. The servers seem to alter data on the relays directly, without any intervening network connection, wireless or otherwise. I suspect some Anomalous form of quantum computing, although I would need to--"

The lighting in the Panopticon suddenly changed. The walls flashed a stoplight red, alternating between bright white and bright red. The familiar feminine voice of the main computer filled the room.

"Severe Anomaly Warning. All personnel Level 4 and higher must respond to this warning."

The Preceptor sighed.

"Hold that thought, Toshi. Don't go too far though in case I need you for this one. Preceptor out."

The Preceptor walked over to the spherical crystal Eye display at the center of the Panopticon. There was a bright splotch of red in the Midwest United States. The audible warning message repeated two more times, then fell silent. The walls, however, continued to flash red periodically. He pulled out his tablet and reviewed the details of the alert.

ANOMALY: Atmospheric Anomaly with Weather Manipulation Signature. LOCATION: Southeast of St. Louis, Missouri, USA.

The Preceptor's pulse quickened. The Eye's global map didn't include small cities, but a quick glance at the growing red splotch confirmed what his intuition was already telling him.

The Anomaly was centered over Gorton, Illinois -- home of Sarah Athraigh.

The Preceptor called the Guardian on his tablet and routed the call through the Panopticon's main speakers.

"Bill, do you see this alert about the Atmospheric Anomaly?"

"On it. What do you need?"

"Do we still have drones on standby in Gorton? Sarah Athraigh's home base?"

"We should. Confirming." The line went silent for a few seconds. "Confirmed. We've got a full drone unit on standby. Surveillance and tactical. Need eyes in the sky?"

"More than eyes, Bill. It's Rory Molan."

"Understood. Deploying the whole unit. Do you have eyes on the target?"

"No. But my intuition tells me he's looking for Sarah Athraigh personally. And this storm is escalating quickly."

The Preceptor zoomed in on the red splotch of Anomalous activity on his tablet. The storm wouldn't look like much on the ground yet, but it had appeared seemingly out of nowhere in a matter of seconds. As he studied the details, the Preceptor turned to confirm that Dr. Bharati was at her desk at the far end of the room.

"Cassandra, how long do we have until this gets ugly?"

Dr. Bharati replied without looking away from her computer.

"If this is Moran, his storms escalate quickly. They also dissipate quickly, so we don't know the full extent of his ability. But each storm is worse than the last."

"Can you give me anything more concrete? When will this one be bad enough to kill people?"

Dr. Bharati's eyes widened. She looked away from her monitor and turned to face the Preceptor.

"It's already starting."

The Preceptor looked back down at his tablet. Gorton

and several surrounding small towns which had been enjoying a sunny day a few minutes ago were now completely covered by an Anomalous thunderstorm.

"Bill, are you with me?"

"Yes, Preceptor."

"Get me eyes on the target. And please, for the good of Order, tell me these drones can handle this weather."

"Will do. They can handle anything short of a hurricane, Truman, but I make no guarantees if this turns into a hurricane. There's no tech this side of the red line that can fly steady in a hurricane." He paused. "Eyes on target. Video feed coming your way."

With a few taps on his tablet, the Preceptor displayed the surveillance drone's video feed on the surface of the Eye. A large rectangle appeared along the equator of the Eye, offering an overhead view of several streets in downtown Gorton, Illinois.

A lone figure was walking down the main street of town. He was a young man with scraggly black hair and beard, wild blue eyes, a black motorcycle jacket, black jeans, black boots, and a sky blue shirt. As he walked down the street, his arms were outstretched with palms facing the sky. His eyes were fixed on the clouds overhead with a look of unbridled joy and childlike wonder.

"Got him. That's definitely Rory Moran."

Rory laughed. The drone had no audio feed, but it was clear from Rory's expression and body language that it must have been raucous laughter. For a moment, the Preceptor thought that Rory looked directly at him through the drone. When Rory turned his attention away from the skies and into the streets, the Preceptor noticed several people approaching Rory.

It was Sarah Athraigh and three of her companions.

The Guardian spoke through the main speakers. "Neutralize target?"

"Not yet. This might be a negotiation. I want to see where this goes."

A tremendous burst of wind and rain surged through the streets of Gorton. The wind knocked Sarah and her companions to the ground but left Rory still standing. The rain started coming down in heavy sheets, and the wind started tugging at everything that wasn't firmly bolted down, tossing trash cans and awnings and a growing flurry of debris in circles through the air.

The Guardian's voice boomed through the speakers.

"Not good, Truman. I can't get a clean shot in these winds. We'll lose the drones eventually."

Sarah rose back to her feet, taking slow but steady steps toward Rory as she shielded her face and eyes from flying debris.

Rory raised his arms high overhead. When he clenched his fists again, lightning started striking repeatedly all around him, filling the street with blinding light. A nearby car exploded, showering shrapnel in a broad radius. Sarah fell down to one knee, barely visible through the driving rain, curling up in a ball to shield herself from flying debris.

The Preceptor threw his tablet at the video feed, clenching his fists and glaring at Rory Moran through the mist.

"I've seen enough. Take out the target."

"Will do. It won't be easy in these winds, though. We may need to light up the whole street."

"Do what you need to do. Just avoid hitting the friendlies. Athraigh and her crew."

There was a long pause.

"Bill?"

"Will do."

The Preceptor watched the scene unfolding on the video feed. The street was littered with debris and scorch marks, but the storm was starting to let up. Sarah and her companions were still crouched defensively on the ground, but the musician, Jonny Glas, seemed to be playing his guitar. Rory was standing dangerously close to Sarah and Hart, the costumed superhero.

Something about the energy of the situation was shifting. Some mix of observation and intuition told the Preceptor that the dynamic on the ground was shifting back into a negotiation.

The Preceptor debated whether or not to rescind the order to neutralize the target. During his moment of hesitation, the drone fired, spraying Rory and the street around him with a hail of bullets. Rory, Hart, and Sarah all fell to the ground.

"Damn it, Bill! Did you hit Athraigh?"

"You're watching the same feed I am, Truman. We'll see in a minute who's still moving."

Rory Moran lay motionless in the street. Sarah Athraigh squirmed out of Hart's restraining grasp, looking around for the shooter.

"She's alive." The Preceptor breathed a sigh of relief. "That answers that question."

"Yes. But she looks pissed."

Sarah glared directly at the camera, clenching her fists at her side. The video feed went blank.

The Guardian's voice boomed over the loudspeakers.

"We lost the feed, Truman. I'm pulling back the rest of the unit. No need to lose more drones because your Anomalous friend there is having a temper tantrum."

The Preceptor sighed.

"Agreed. I'll let you know if I need you for anything else, Bill. Preceptor out."

The Preceptor turned to Dr. Bharati, who was staring at the Eye with a stunned expression.

"How's the storm looking, Cassandra?"

Dr. Bharati blinked, looking back down at her monitor.

"I still see evidence of the storm, but the intensity seems to be diminishing. I suspect it will dissipate on its own fairly quickly now that the source of the disturbance has been... neutralized."

"Yes, let's hope so. And even though he's been neutralized, I still need you to analyze this storm carefully and add an additional report to his file. Studying his Anomalous ability may help us to understand and respond to other weather manipulators."

"Yes, Preceptor. I'll have a report for you within the next forty-eight hours"

"Excellent. Thank you."

The Preceptor closed the empty video feed and stared at the Eye. The red splotch southeast of St. Louis was still there, but it seemed to have faded and changed color slightly, like a bruise in the process of healing. The storm itself was all but over -- but the strangeness of it, and the economic damage left in its wake, would destabilize the region for some time.

He reached out and touched the Anomalous spot with his index finger. It felt no different than the rest of the cool surface of the crystal sphere, but his hand lingered there anyway as he contemplated the spot's significance.

His intuition told him that the Anomalous energy Rory Moran had brought into the world was a sneak preview of what was coming.

CHAPTER 19

The Preceptor sat in the telepresence room across from the Guardian. The Guardian's telepresence theme featured walls with simple but elegant solid mahogany panelling and polished white marble with gold veins that gave the room the look and feel of a dignified home study or possibly the office of a dignitary at a prestigious academic or financial institution.

The two men stared at each other in silence. Eventually, the Preceptor spoke.

"Did you target Sarah Athraigh?"

"No."

"Bill, if you did this, you need to level with me. I can handle it, but you need to level with me. Did you--"

"No. Rory Moran was the only target. We engaged the target while he was in close quarters with several other people. The drone was subjected to hurricane-speed gusts of wind. My operator took the necessary steps to neutralize the target. Athraigh was caught in the line of fire."

"Did you instruct your operators to avoid hitting my assets?"

There was a long pause. When it was clear that the Guardian wasn't answering, the Preceptor picked up his tablet.

"One of my assets took fire that would have been fatal if he weren't a fast-healing freak wearing a bulletproof superhero costume. And he took that fire because your operator nearly killed the woman who may well be the most important asset we have in the most important operation of Order right now."

The Guardian rolled his eyes and sighed. The Preceptor cringed, clenching his fists.

"Oh, you disagree?"

"The Sovereign disagrees. He instructed me to disregard Athraigh's status as a protected Order asset and anything else you've got going on with that damned Favorable Anomalies scenario of yours. I didn't target her, but I didn't protect her either. She should be thankful her cosplayer friend was there to take a bullet for her. She may not be so lucky next time."

The Preceptor stood up, placing the knuckles of his clenched fists on the table.

"And since when is it the Sovereign's place to micro-manage the details of Order's operations?"

"It's not operations, Truman. It's policy. Favorable Anomalies is out. Your continued obsession with a rejected scenario is a fool's errand at best. Out of Order at worst. I can't stop you, but I won't go down with you."

"Favorable Anomalies isn't out, Bill. The Sovereign instructed me to accept his depopulation scenario as a viable outcome. I did. I do accept it, in all sincerity. I accept that we may ultimately have to stay the course with Order while the vast majority of humanity falls. I'm doing everything I can to prepare for that eventuality. That doesn't mean it's the only possible solution to the problem, much less the best one."

"You need to talk that over with the Sovereign, then. The way he tells it, Athraigh and her crew are a dangerous distraction, along with the whole Favorable Anomalies scenario. If the world's really going to burn, we need to start prepping, not put up some solar panels and sing Kumbaya around the campfire."

"I am preparing, Bill. That's exactly what I'm doing. And I will speak with the Sovereign about this. Preceptor out."

The Preceptor closed the connection. The walls, floor, and ceiling faded to their bright white default setting. He grabbed his tablet and stormed out of the telepresence room, already mentally composing his next message to the Sovereign.

The Preceptor sat at his desk in the Panopticon, reading the full report about yesterday's incident in Gorton, Illinois.

Rory Moran's death had been confirmed. His body was en route to Inquisitorium Prime for further study. Sarah Athraigh and her companions sustained only minor injuries -- with the exception of Hart, who was probably seriously injured by the drone strike, but showed little sign of it today due to his Anomalous self-healing ability. They were all currently engaging in various disaster relief efforts in Gorton, which was still without power or passable roads in the aftermath of the Anomalous storm.

The most concerning development was a video recently uploaded by Sarah Athraigh calling for an Eutopia Assembly in New York at the end of October. The date was set to coincide with the International Conference on Climate Economics. This meant that momentum around the Eutopia Engine project was escalating -- and would be drawing a crowd of highly Anomalous individuals into New York City at the same time that many prominent political and business leaders were gathering nearby for a climate conference.

The Preceptor leaned back in his chair and sighed. Much like the Eutopia Engine itself, this event would be a dangerous mix of opportunity for change and potential for disaster. After reviewing the latest update on the Eutopia Engine, he opened up a video chat with the Insight.

"Good morning, Insight."

"Good morning, Preceptor. I wasn't expecting to hear from you this morning. How can I help you?"

"I just reviewed the report on yesterday's incident in Gorton and I'm concerned about this new Eutopia Assembly concept that Athraigh's pushing. I know it's only been a few hours, but do you have any strategic analysis of this potential threat yet?"

"That's what I was just working on now, actually."

"Good. You're ahead of the game then."

The Insight smiled. "I do what I can."

"What do you have so far?"

"Let's see." She paused, reviewing her notes on her tablet. "Unfortunately, it's mostly bad news. The good news is that it may in fact increase pressure on attendees at the climate conference to adopt a more proactive and effective approach to climate adaptation and mitigation. The bad news, though, is that it will likely be too much pressure, and the wrong kind of pressure."

The Preceptor nodded. "My thoughts exactly."

"Yes. And what little data we have so far about this Eutopia Engine project backs up our suspicions. Some of the most vocal participants in the alpha test were Order-aware AR militants who plan to use the Eutopia Engine to overthrow and replace Order. The new wave of participants joining the new beta test aren't as Order-aware, but they're just as eager to see this Eutopia project replace key functions of government and business with a decentralized network of individuals and small groups who plan and implement public policy autonomously."

The Preceptor shook his head.

"But humanity's not ready for that. That's why we have governments instead of running everything by referendum. The average citizen can barely be trusted to balance a checkbook or pick between two candidates that we spoon feed them. Turning all of the power over to the masses through some electronic direct democracy scheme would be disastrous."

"Exactly. And my concern here -- which I was just writing about in my analysis, actually -- is that this Eutopia Assembly will be a step too far. As long as it's just something they do online, it's not that big of a deal. They'll view it like any other social network they belong to, and we can spin it however we like. But once they start meeting face-to-face, claiming physical spaces, talking about serious issues that affect them personally--"

"Then it becomes something that's as real to them as their local government, if not more so."

"Yes. You see the problem, then."

"Yes." The Preceptor sighed. "How's this going to affect the Favorable Anomalies scenario? One way or another, we're going to have to intervene in some way in this Eutopia Engine and Eutopia Assembly. But this must be handled delicately. We need to preserve the integrity of Order, but at the same time I wouldn't want to jeopardize the--"

The Preceptor paused. He was receiving a video chat request from the Sovereign.

"Hold that thought. I've got the Sovereign on the other line."

The Preceptor accepted the video chat request from the Sovereign. The Sovereign appeared to be calling from the back seat of a limousine rather than a secure Order location, which would have been the proper protocol for all official Order business.

"Good morning, Sovereign. What--"

"No time to chat, Truman. I need to talk to you immediately about this Eutopia Assembly business, and a few other things. And it needs to be in person. Meet me at my home base immediately. I'm stuck in traffic leaving the city, so if you leave now by air, you may beat me there."

"I--"

"Sovereign out."

The video chat ended. The Preceptor stared at the empty window for a moment, then remembered that he was still on video chat with the Insight. He switched back over to her window.

"Sorry, Kendra, I have to go. The Sovereign wants to meet with me in person."

The color drained from the Insight's face.

"Is it serious? Does he know that you know about his... secret?"

"It's something serious, but I don't think he knows. It's about the Eutopia Assembly, and something else he didn't go into detail about. The fact that he wants to meet in person seems to indicate that it's not going to be a pleasant conversation"

 "Yes. I'll let you get to it, then." She paused. "Be careful, Truman."

 "I will."

 "And tell me how it goes."

 "I will."

 "Good. I look forward to it. For the Victory of Order."

 "For the Victory of Order."

CHAPTER 20

The Preceptor's black helicopter touched down on one of several concrete helipads at the small airfield on the south side of the Sovereign's private residence in upstate New York. He had heard rumors over the years that the illustrious Percival Sword lived in an extravagant fortified bunker when he wasn't busy jetting around the world for business and pleasure, but he had never had any reason to visit the site or investigate the details. Now, as he approached the main entrance to the compound, he made a mental note to do some more research.

Castle Sword had the look and feel of a Cold War era take on a medieval castle. It featured a classic concentric castle design with a broad moat, low outer curtain wall, outer ward, high inner curtain wall, and inner ward. The almost perfect symmetry of the design reminded the Preceptor of Beaumaris Castle, although the basic design concept could have been inspired by any number of other castles. The walls all appeared to be made of reinforced concrete which the Preceptor suspected was further reinforced by exotic materials. Each of the two concentric rings of walls featured four large towers and four smaller towers in a roughly octagonal shape, distended slightly on the north and south sides of the inner wall by the presence of large gatehouses.

The Preceptor stopped at the near end of the steel drawbridge, admiring the architecture while the dozen members of his security detail took their positions in a semicircle around him. They were all wearing full Champion field gear -- black body armor, assault rifle at high ready, thin black gloves, black helmet, big black headphones, and thick black goggles. The two security guards who approached the Preceptor in simple black uniforms with ballistic vests and visorless helmets seemed underdressed by comparison.

"Doctor Truman Stuart?"

The Preceptor gave the two young men a curious look. Their manner of addressing him confirmed his initial suspicion. These men were private contractors, not Initiates of Order.

"Yes."

"Mr. Sword is expecting you. Please follow me."

The Preceptor stepped forward. When his security detail proceeded to follow him, the guard held out a hand to stop them.

"Just you."

The Preceptor shook his head. "This is my first time visiting this facility. My security detail goes with me wherever I go."

"Mr. Sword has only granted clearance for you, sir."

"Then ask him to grant clearance for my security detail, or I will. I'm not going in alone."

The security guard took a few steps away from the Preceptor and spoke into a walkie talkie.

"He's here, sir, but he wants to bring in his whole security detail."

After a brief pause, the guard looked around at the Initiates surrounding the Preceptor.

"Twelve, sir. They look a lot like one of your special units. Rifles, tactical goggles, headphones."

There was a longer pause.

"Understood."

The guard turned back to the Preceptor.

"He'll meet you in the outer ward. Follow me."

The Preceptor and his security detail followed the two guards across the steel drawbridge and through the outer gate. After walking through a long, narrow entryway, they reached a large open area between the outer and inner walls. A broad stone footpath meandered through this open area between the two walls, bordered on either side by a blend of mosses and a variety of blue, green, and white ground cover plants.

The guard pointed down the path.

"Mr. Sword is on his way up. He'll meet you at the second door on your right."

The two guards walked over to a small doorway at the edge of the entryway, disappearing inside. After looking around for another moment, the Preceptor walked along the weathered grey stones of the path through the outer ward. His security detail followed suit, staying on the stones to avoid trampling the verdant moss along the edges. Just as the Preceptor was passing the first small steel door on his right, he saw the Sovereign stepping out from a second door farther down the path.

"Truman! Welcome to my not-so-humble abode. I see you've brought a few friends with you."

The two men stopped within arms length of each other. The Preceptor glanced back at the twelve members of his security detail who were spread out evenly along the stone path behind him.

"Yes. It's customary for me to bring a security detail to any location not directly controlled by Order."

The Sovereign laughed.

"Cut the bullshit, Truman. It's a show of force -- as is my refusal to allow them access to the inner ward and bunker. We're in a pissing contest, you and I. Walk with me and we'll see if we can talk this out."

The Sovereign turned and started walking away down the stone path. The Preceptor motioned for his security detail to wait here, then followed the Sovereign down the path, catching up to walk beside him as they spoke.

"Tell me, Truman. What do you think about this Eutopia Assembly business?"

"It's concerning."

"Concerning. Elaborate."

"It has the potential to be the start of something that could quickly spiral out of our control. Most of it seems benign for now -- reducing emissions, feeding the hungry, local philanthropy, that sort of thing. But the most active organizers seem to have a decidedly anti-Order perspective. And between the decentralization and the Anomalous information technology, we have no quick and easy way to intervene in the course of the project. Assembling in person will cement this project as a real-world phenomenon rather than just another pie-in-the-sky idea floating around in digital reality."

"My thoughts exactly, Truman. Now tell me -- what's your Favorable Anomaly been up to lately? This Sarah Athraigh character?"

The Preceptor sighed. "We believe she and her people are among the leader organizers of the Eutopia Engine and the Assembly, if that's what you're getting at. They've also--"

The Sovereign held up a hand to interrupt the Preceptor.

"And she herself was the one who first announced the organizing of this Eutopia Assembly, yes?"

"Yes."

"Good. You understand the situation we find ourselves in, then."

"The situation we find ourselves in is that Favorable Anomalies is still the scenario with the best projected outcome for the largest number of people, and Sarah Athraigh is--"

The Sovereign stopped walking. The Preceptor stopped talking and followed suit, stopping just a few feet away, facing the Sovereign. The two men stared at each other in silence for a long moment before the Sovereign spoke.

"Favorable Anomalies is a fool's errand, Truman. You can't go around supporting a bunch of Anomalous militants like Athraigh and then act surprised when they back Anomalous projects like this Eutopia business that pose an existential threat to Order. That's like giving matches to a child and complaining when they burn down the house. It's not the child's fault, it's your fault."

The Preceptor clenched his fists, twisting his head and curling his lips as he drew breath with a slight hiss.

"Have you looked at the data, Percival? I know you've read the executive summaries, but have you really studied the data? I have -- and it keeps me up at night."

The Preceptor took a step toward the Sovereign, glaring directly at him with less than a foot of space between them.

"You advocate rapid depopulation, but you seem to have a sanitized notion of what the deaths of seven billion people in a single generation would look like. The people you so charmingly refer to as 'maladapted humans' don't simply fade quietly out of existence. A global conflagration erupts that will result in the untimely death of almost all human beings. And Order may not endure the resulting chaos. Surely you see that."

"What do the projections say, Truman?"

"I--"

"The projections say that Order will endure!" The Sovereign laughed, patting the Preceptor on the shoulder. "As it always has, as it always will. Call the loss of seven billion surplus humans a tragedy if you will. I, for one, will shed no tears for them. The best, the brightest, the strongest among us, will emerge from this evolutionary bottleneck with far more room to breathe on this tiny piece of rock we call home -- and an entire cosmos to explore once we're no longer wasting so much time and resources shepherding seven billion cattle!"

The Preceptor shook his head. "There's still enough time for the majority of humanity to live. If you trust the models to project a smooth depopulation, then trust them to project a smooth application of the Favorable Anomalies scenario."

The Sovereign dismissed the Preceptor's concerns with a wave of his hand.

"Nonsense. This Eutopia business is proof positive that you've gone too far with that approach. You had your chance, and these Anomalous militants proved themselves to be what they always have been and always will be -- incorrigible malcontents who will never rest until they've torn down everything Order has sought to build."

"I--"

"Now listen here, Truman. Here's what we're going to do."

The Sovereign lowered his voice to a whisper, leaning in closer to speak near the Preceptor's right ear.

"We're going to let them have their Eutopia Assembly. And we're going to use it as an opportunity to draw them out into the open. Raid the assembly, round up the organizers, track down every remotely Anomalous person we can find and lock them up in a tiny room somewhere -- or better yet, in a box. This may be our best chance in decades to crush Anomalous Revolution and its allies -- and by God, we're taking it."

The two men stared at each other for a long moment. Eventually, the Preceptor broke the silence.

"All Anomalies?"

"Yes, all Anomalies. I--"

Something in the Sovereign's expression shifted. His smooth, commanding tone of voice and presence faltered. The Preceptor suddenly felt dissected under the calculating glare of his sharp blue eyes.

The Sovereign didn't seem to be able to manipulate the Preceptor's mind -- but the Preceptor realized with a chill that he might be able to read it. Even if he couldn't, he could probably guess where the conversation was leading.

"Consider your next words carefully, Truman. Very carefully."

"I suggest you do the same."

The Sovereign glared at the Preceptor. The Preceptor felt a sudden rush as he realized that the Sovereign was trying to manipulate his mind. The air around them tingled with the electric tension between them. He felt a passing whim to just go along with the Sovereign's plan, which he suspected was related to this Anomalous mental push. But it wasn't a serious thought, and it didn't take hold.

After a few seconds, the Sovereign took a step back, his face flushed with anger.

"This thing you think you know about me, Truman. It

doesn't matter anymore. Under my plan, all Anomalies who surrender willingly and swear allegiance to Order will be granted amnesty and protected Prodigy status."

"How convenient."

"Yes, actually. It will also accelerate the evolution of human consciousness by fully embracing all exceptional individuals who choose the path of Order. You see, Truman? Everyone wins."

"Everyone except the seven billion who lose."

The Sovereign sighed, throwing his hands up in exasperation..

"There you are, on about that again.We're clearly never going to agree on that point, are we? But here's the thing. We've got at least another decade or two until the worst of it, yes?"

The Preceptor crossed his arms, glaring at the Sovereign.

"The worst of it, yes. But it's already--"

"But you see? We can worry about, say, six of those seven billion in another decade or two. We can keep having these little philosophical debates over tea every few months for the next few decades. In the meantime, you and I have more in common with each other than we do with those Anomalous rabble-rousers, yes? We both agree that the Eutopia Engine and Eutopia Assembly are too dangerous to overlook?"

The Preceptor hesitated. As he mulled over the question, he was confident that the Sovereign wasn't using his Anomalous ability to manipulate his mind. And yet, he found himself agreeing.

"Yes."

"There we have it!" The Sovereign clapped his hands together in excitement. "There's the Truman Stuart I've heard about whose devotion to Order is second to none! Focus on the task at hand. See that this Eutopia business is taken care of. Maybe when the dust settles, this little disagreement of ours will find its resolution."

The Sovereign turned and started walking away. When the Preceptor realized that he was leaving, he started following him down the stone path.

"This isn't the end of it, Percival."

"It is for now."

The Sovereign reached the door that he had emerged from and pulled it open. As he was about to step inside, a thought occurred to the Preceptor.

"My predecessor. Derek Lichtenberg. Why did he choose to speak to the Fae?"

The Sovereign froze, clasping the handle of the door tightly.

"What do you mean?"

"I mean that something led him to speak in person, one-on-one, with a Fae creature. The Guardian doesn't seem to know why. Derek's personal notes and task manager, which I inherited, don't offer any clues. What led him to travel out to the middle of nowhere with just a handful of Initiates to speak to this powerful Fae creature? Do you have any idea?"

The Sovereign hesitated.

"He was searching for answers to some fundamental questions about the nature of Order and the reasons why so many Anomalous beings and factions stand in opposition to it."

"I see. And what happened to him?"

The Sovereign paused, averting his eyes.

"He found what he was looking for."

Without another word, the Sovereign opened the door and disappeared inside. The Preceptor stood there for a moment, staring at the door and contemplating the Sovereign's last words. Eventually, he turned around and led his security detail back to the main gate.

CHAPTER 21

The Preceptor sat at a desk at New York Keep's Emergency Command Center. It was a large room with two dozen steel desks, a wide variety of different computers and displays, and a blank white wall at the front of the room that served as a giant main viewscreen. Several smaller screens on either side of the main viewscreen provided supplemental information. The room was filled with dozens of Initiates at their desks in business casual civilian garb. Another dozen Initiates in full Champion gear guarded the four exits to the room, in spite of the fact that they were all gathered at the heart at one of the most secure Order locations in the world, second only to the Panopticon.

"Truman! I see you're making yourself at home in my old stomping grounds."

The Preceptor turned around to see the Guardian entering the room. He rose from his seat and walked over to greet him, offering a polite handshake.

"Bill Lamont, in the flesh. It's been ages since we've actually met in person, hasn't it?"

"Yes. Too long. Glad to see you're on board with the operation today."

The Preceptor smirked. "I helped plan the operation, Bill. Of course I'm on board."

"You know what I mean, Truman." The Guardian lowered his voice, leaning forward slightly. "Your disagreement with the Sovereign."

"Ah, yes. We still haven't settled that disagreement. But we agree that Eutopia is a threat to Order. That's enough for today."

"And what about Athraigh?"

"Sarah Athraigh still has a role to play in the Favorable Anomalies scenario. What that role is remains to be seen."

"It might involve spending a long time in a small room -- or a smaller box."

"We'll see how the day goes, Bill. The Anomalous are by their very nature unpredictable. They may find a solution that none of us anticipated."

The Preceptor returned to his desk at the front of the room. The Guardian soon joined him at another computer just a few seats away.

The main viewscreen was filled with live aerial view of most of Manhattan. Two locations were highlighted with large green circles: the Javits Convention Center, venue for the Eutopia Assembly, and Madison Square Garden, venue for the International Conference on Climate Economics.

Since the two venues were less than a mile apart, the Preceptor's biggest concern at the moment was that the fairly mainstream and nonviolent demonstrators outside of the ICCE could easily be radicalized by the more Anomalous attendees at the Eutopia Assembly. That risk would escalate dramatically once the raids on the Eutopia Assembly and other select Anomalous sites began. Desperate Anomalous militants fleeing the raid might try to turn a whole slice of Manhattan from the Hudson to the Empire State Building into a violent uprising, complete with psychokinetic car-flinging, spontaneous explosions, and who knows what other outbursts of Anomalous disruption.

The forces of Order had to be prepared for any eventuality -- and keep the activity at the two sites separate for as long as possible.

While the Preceptor was studying the map and reviewing the details of the Eutopia raid, another symbol appeared on the map -- a white crown surrounded by a white circle.

The Sovereign.

As the crown moved toward Madison Square Garden, the Preceptor's brow furrowed. The Sovereign was scheduled to speak at the ICCE -- but he was arriving much earlier than planned. A quick review of the Sovereign's updated itinerary indicated that he had rescheduled his trip so that he would arrive at ICCE before the Eutopia raid rather than after. He had also tripled the size of his security detail, which now included thirty-six Initiates of Order in full Champion gear.

The Preceptor felt his pulse quicken as a rush of intuition confirmed that something was wrong. The Sovereign was planning some dramatic intervention that would threaten the entire Favorable Anomalies scenario.

"Bill." The Preceptor rose from his seat. "I'm going out in the field."

The Guardian turned and gave the Preceptor a blank stare.

"I... what? You've got to be kidding me."

"I'm not kidding, Bill. I'm going out in the field."

"But..." The Guardian waved his arms around the room in exasperation. "Look at all of this data about what's going on out in the field! And these thick reinforced concrete walls, protected by extra layers of exotic materials and a veritable army of Initiates sworn to guard you with their very lives! Why would you leave that all behind and put yourself in the line of fire?"

The whole room suddenly became quiet. The Guardian looked around and sighed, stepping within arms length of the Preceptor and lowering his voice to a near whisper.

"Look, don't get me wrong. I'm impressed by your penchant for field work. You rose through the ranks of Order as a number-crunching desk jockey, and now you're a hands-on Preceptor, out in the field every chance you get. I didn't see that coming. The Sovereign sure as hell didn't see that coming. But today is not the day, Truman! Who knows what those people are about to unleash on the streets of this city?"

The Preceptor shook his head.

"'Those people' think they're attending a peaceful and largely uneventful conference about their favorite do-gooder causes. Their response to the raid will be reactive, largely predictable, and easily contained. What I'm more concerned about is my Preceptor's intuition telling me that something strange is going down at ICCE."

The Guardian hesitated. "ICCE?"

"Yes." The Preceptor pointed to the main screen. "The Sovereign's there early with a large contingent of Champions. He clearly thinks something big's about to go down. I tend to agree with him."

The Guardian stepped back to his computer, reviewing the details of the Sovereign's updated itinerary.

"You're right." He studied his computer for a few more moments, then turned back to the Preceptor. "All the more reason for you to stay put. The fewer targets in the line of fire, the better. You can--"

"I'm not asking your permission, Bill. I can do more out there than I can in here. I'm going." He pointed to one of the two green circles on the main viewscreen. "You take point on the raid on Eutopia Assembly and all of the police and private contractors we're coordinating through Homeland Security. I'll take point on the security detail at ICCE and anything else that goes down at Madison Square Garden. I'll keep a line open to you at all times. Let me know any major updates on your end and I'll do the same."

"Will do. Stay safe out there, Truman."

"I will."

The Guardian sat back down at his computer. The Preceptor closed down everything on his computer and headed for the exit.

Police barricades surrounded Madison Square Garden. Several checkpoints limited flow of foot traffic into the Garden to people with delegate or media access to the International Conference on Climate Economics. .

The Preceptor marched on the Garden with a security detail of thirty-six Initiates of Order in full Champion field gear -- black body armor, assault rifle at high ready, thin black gloves, black helmets, big black headphones, and thick black goggles. The Preceptor himself was also dressed in full Champion gear minus the rifle. The goggles and headphones were clipped to his belt, and a bold white "O" was emblazoned on his ballistic vest. He didn't wear the Champion gear often, but like all upper-level Initiates of Order, he had full training in the special tools and tactics Champions used to respond to various Anomalous phenomena.

When they reached the checkpoint at the main entrance, the Preceptor presented his Homeland Security credentials and spoke to the commanding officer. After a brief discussion of logistics, the Preceptor led his security detail into the Garden and stationed them on one side of the foyer. The police continued to maintain the main barricades and checkpoints, while the Preceptor's detail simply monitored the crowd inside and outside for any Anomalous behavior and awaited further orders from the Preceptor.

The Preceptor took a few steps away from his security detail and tapped a button on his vest to mute his audio connection with the Guardian. He pulled out his tablet and opened up a video chat with the Insight.

"Good morning, Insight."

"Good morning, Preceptor." The Insight smiled. "My, don't you look dashing in your Champion gear."

The Preceptor smirked. "Hardly. I haven't worn it in ages. I feel a bit like a child playing dress-up. But it's the best body armor known to modern science, so I'll take it."

"It suits you." Her expression grew more serious. "How can I help you?"

"I need you to help me figure out what the Sovereign's up to. He arrived here hours ahead of schedule with a team of Champions. It's a power play of some sort, but I want to know details before it happens."

"Got it."

The Insight started typing and looking slightly to the side. After a few moments she started nodding to herself.

"Yes, here it is. I don't know exactly what he's up to, but it's got to be a social engineering op. He's spent the past twenty-four hours communicating heavily with the Catalyst and a few key personnel on his news network, PEN News." She paused. "Is he just doing damage control for the upcoming raid?"

"No, it's more than that. He would have coordinated with us if it were that simple." The Preceptor paused, raising his free hand and listening in silence for any hints of intuition. "He wants to start a public war against Anomalous Revolution."

"Public? As in--"

"As in publicly declaring them a terrorist organization and mobilizing world governments to move against them. PEN News already has the press releases. They're just waiting for the raid to start. I can feel the information starting to spread already."

The Insight's eyes widened.

"But... how can he do that without the public finding out about the Anomalous abilities some of these AR militants have?"

"He can't." The Preceptor cringed, clenching his free hand. "I don't think he cares anymore. It's all going to be public now. Maybe he'll even make Order public. Whatever it takes to put an end to the Favorable Anomalies scenario and advance his depopulation approach."

The Insight shook her head.

"That's too far."

"Yes."

The Preceptor paused, considering his options. He glanced at the time and realized that the raid on the Eutopia Assembly was going to start at any minute.

"Run a few tests on the metamodel to see how the Sovereign's actions will affect our top scenarios. And Contact the Council of Order. See if they know about his plans to go public.

If they do, there's not much we can do. But if they don't... tell them what we know about the Sovereign."

"Everything?"

"Everything."

"Understood. I'll contact them right away." She paused. "What will you be doing?"

"Keeping an eye on things here at the ICCE -- and hopefully having a word with the Sovereign."

"Be careful, Truman."

"You too. For the Victory of Order."

"For the Victory of Order."

The Preceptor put away his tablet and unmuted his connection to the Guardian.

"Bill, are you there?"

He heard a familiar voice in the small earpiece he was wearing on his left ear.

"Yes, Truman."

"Has the Eutopia raid started yet?"

"It's starting as we speak."

The Preceptor sighed. "Can you get me an exact location for the Sovereign? I'm in the foyer at the Garden now. Where is he?"

There was a long pause.

"He should be in the Theater upstairs."

"Thanks, Bill."

"Is something wrong, Truman?"

"I'll let you know, Bill. Preceptor out."

The Preceptor muted his connection with the Guardian, motioned for half of his security detail to follow him, and headed upstairs.

The Theater at Madison Square Garden was a spacious venue capable of seating several thousand people. Several hundred people were currently seated on the main floor of the theatre, listening attentively to a woman speaking up on the stage. As soon as the Preceptor entered, several Initiates of Order in full Champion gear stopped him near the door.

The Preceptor raised his hand, motioning for his own security detail to wait in the doorway. He glared at one of the Champions who was detaining him.

"You do know who I am, don't you?"

The Champion's smooth black goggles stared back at him blankly.

"Yes, Preceptor. The Sovereign instructed us to intercept you. He will speak with you in the lobby."

The Preceptor cringed, clenching his fists in anger. He took a deep breath and let it out slowly. Before he could re-spond, he heard a familiar voice.

"Relax, Truman. No need to create a scene. Let's step out-side."

The Sovereign approached him from the nearest aisle. When he reached the Preceptor, the two men stepped out into the lobby.

"What seems to be the problem, Truman?"

The Preceptor glared at the Sovereign.

"You know very well what the problem is. You're about to turn this operation into a public war against Anomalous Revolution."

"Well, there you have it." The Sovereign laughed. "You've got me. You figured that out sooner than I thought you would!" He pointed to the stage. "I thought you'd find out about it on the big screen over there just like everyone else. Here you are, a few minutes early, come to complain to me about it."

"This isn't a game, Percival. You can't just--"

"Tell me, Truman. Do you still support the cause of Order?"

"Yes. I--"

"And do you still think the Eutopia Engine is a threat to Order?"

The Preceptor paused.

"In its current form, yes. Definitely. Humanity simply isn't ready to govern itself yet. It needs the guiding hand of Order to steer it in the right direction. But--"

"Precisely!" The Sovereign clasped his hands together. "And Anomalous Revolution isn't going to give up on this Eutopia business now that it's started. They're like a dog with a bone. They'll never let it go. The only solution is to strike hard and fast, right now, against all the Anomalous, before it's too late."

"Too late for Order? Or too late for your visions of rapid depopulation?"

The Sovereign sighed in exasperation.

"You're starting to sound like one of them, Truman!" He pointed to the Preceptor's tablet, which was hanging in a holster from his belt. "Do your job or your job will be taken from you. Finish the raid -- and keep all of the Anomalous fanatics out of this conference."

"All of them? Every last person with an Anomalous belief or ability?"

The Sovereign glared at the Preceptor.

"Goodbye, Truman."

The Sovereign turned around and walked back into the Theater.

The Preceptor shook his head and started walking back down to the foyer, motioning for his security detail to follow. He hadn't gotten very far when he heard Bill's voice through his earpiece.

"Truman, are you there?"

The Preceptor unmuted his connection to the Guardian and continued walking toward the foyer.

"Yes. What is it?"

"Some Eutopia targets are headed your way. We've got most of them contained at Javits, but a few clusters made it out. Check your map. You've got to see this."

The Preceptor pulled out his tablet and looked at the live overhead view of the target area between the Javits Conference Center and Madison Square Garden. There were several red circles in the streets between the two venues. Most of the circles highlighted obvious flashes of lights or flickers of motion and were accompanied by small automated text that attempted to identify the nature of the disturbance: psychokinesis; pyrokinesis; electrokinesis; physical violence that may or may not involve any specialized Anomalous abilities.

"That's a lot, Bill. How did so many of them escape the raid?"

"No idea. They must have been out in the streets before we even moved on Javits. Either someone tipped them off or they got a memo from their little Psychic Friends Network. Either way, we've got an ugly mess on our hands here." The Guardian sighed. "Is it time to deploy the LAWS? I have a four dozen LAWS units and a few dozen other tactical robots on standby."

The Preceptor studied the red circles and notes on his tablet. There were numerous disturbances, but there were also still a large number of police and Initiates of Order between Javits and the Garden.

"Not yet, Bill. Shut down the cell towers and control the crowd with the nonlethals and drone strikes as needed. But don't send out the LAWS until I say so. We haven't had to deploy them in a civilian context yet. I'd like to keep it that way." He paused. "If you lose contact with me though, go ahead. Their resistance to mind effects may come in handy."

"Will do."

The Preceptor reached the foyer and rejoined the other half of his security detail. When he looked outside, he noticed that the crowd of demonstrators visible from the foyer had doubled in the short time he'd spent talking to the Sovereign.

He checked his tablet for any updates. There were actually fewer red circles than before, which was a comforting sign. But they were all closer to the Garden than before, and one of them was new and flashing.

Drone Compromised. Deactivated.

"Bill, you still there?"

"Yes."

"I need eyes on whatever just took out one of our drones."

"Already on it. Sending more drones and Champions to

the drone's last known location."

The Preceptor studied the tactical map on his tablet. Several of the small dots representing Order's drones converged on a spot near the barricades surrounding the Garden. He selected one and viewed the live video feed.

The drone provided a near street-level view of a large section of the crowd demonstrating around the barricades at the Garden. Clouds of teargas and pepper spray wafted through the air as hundreds of people responded in chaotic but somewhat predictable ways to the potent mix of airborne chemicals, flashbang grenades, and sound cannons that the police and Order were deploying against the nonviolent majority gathered in the streets. Most of the people were retreating, either falling back to regroup or leaving the scene entirely down side streets. Some were still advancing against the crowd, outnumbered and outgunned by the large police presence. Crowd control procedures were starting to bring the situation back under control, dispersing the less militant demonstrators and containing the more militant ones.

And then, everything changed.

The Preceptor's eyes widened as a large segment of the crowd -- hundreds of people -- all stopped in place at the same moment and started looking around at each other in confusion. After a few seconds, they all started moving slowly and calmly toward the barricades in unison. One of the sound cannons -- a large truck equipped with a large dish that broadcast disorienting sounds to disperse crowds -- moved along with the crowd to the edge of the barricade. The riot police held their ground briefly, then eventually lowered their weapons and stepped aside, allowing the demonstrators to pass through a large opening forming in the barricade.

The Preceptor cringed, clenching his fist and glaring at the tablet.

"Oh, no you don't."

He strode toward the main entrance, motioning for his security detail to follow.

"Champions of Order! We have a large Anomalous crowd approaching. Target the sound cannon and keep an eye out for any Anomalies who may be using tech or mind abilities to direct the crowd. Go!"

The blackclad Champions marched forward ahead of the Preceptor, pouring out of the foyer and into the streets in front of the Garden. As he stepped through the front doors, the Preceptor heard the sound cannon broadcasting a song about peace.

"Peace, Salaam, Shalom."

The Champions fired on the sound cannon with live rounds, striking it repeatedly at close range and eventually shorting out the entire sound system. As the music screeched to a halt, they formed a defensive line in front of the entrance to the Garden, keeping the crowd at bay with raised rifles and a clear readiness to use them.

The Preceptor stepped forward to scan the crowd. A chill ran down his spine when he saw who was at the head of the crowd.

Sarah Athraigh.

Sarah and her companions were all gathered in front of the Preceptor's line of Champions. Like a good field tactician, she was quickly surveying the sudden shift in her surroundings and assessing her options. Once she realized that the Champions were a primary -- and likely insurmountable -- obstacle, she crossed her arms and glared at them, glancing at the growing number of drones circling over her head.

The Preceptor grabbed a bullhorn from one of the police officers on the barricade who had stepped aside to make way for Sarah and her companions. He muted his connection to the Guardian, then turned on the bullhorn and pointed it in Sarah's direction.

"Sarah Athraigh, please step forward."

Sarah stared at him blankly. He thought he caught a flicker of recognition on her face, but couldn't otherwise determine what exactly she was thinking.

"You heard me, Sarah. Please step forward."

Sarah glared at the Preceptor. "How about you tell your soldiers to stand down?"

"No."

He paused, scanning his surroundings carefully. The crowd seemed to be back under control now that the Anomalous music had stopped playing. The police on the front lines were coming back to their senses and looking to the Preceptor and his Champions for guidance on how to proceed.

"I will, however, give you some breathing room. Gentlemen, fall back and guard the entrance."

As the Preceptor's line of Champions marched backward, the Preceptor stepped forward, giving one of them his bullhorn and slipping between them to approach Sarah. Sarah also stepped forward, meeting the Preceptor halfway between her companions and the entrance to the building.

For a few moments, the two stood within arm's length of each other, staring at each other in silence. Eventually, Sarah was the first to speak.

"Is this the part where you tell me that I'm a valuable but replaceable asset?"

The Preceptor smiled.

"No, Sarah. Not you. You are the reason Order exists. You are a brilliant human being capable of advancing the evolution of human consciousness beyond anything that most people can dream of. The musty old men who currently rule the world are but a prelude to the reality that you and your spiritual kin will create."

Sarah looked at him with genuine confusion.

"Then why are you standing in my way?"

"The world isn't ready."

The Preceptor drew his handgun out of its holster on his belt, running his gloved fingertips over the cool steel affectionately.

"Eutopia Engine. The synergistic combination of political action, information technology, and arcane arts in the service of direct democracy. Detailed, viable, and increasingly popular plans to reform election laws and restructure national and global economies. In a matter of months, you and your little band of magical misfits have inspired millions of people to believe that they have the power and the right to change the world as they see fit. You've brought us far closer to a global revolution than you even realize."

Sarah shook her head with a smile and a chuckle.

"Isn't that a good thing? Isn't that the way to solve climate change and all the other major problems in the world today? Get a bunch of people to put their heads together and come up with the best solutions for everyone?"

"No."

The Preceptor looked over his shoulder, then looked over Sarah's shoulder, his sharp blue eyes scanning the hundreds of faces that surrounded them.

"The masses aren't ready to design their own future. Not yet. Why are all of these people here today, Sarah? My people are here because I ordered them to be here. Your people are here because a handful of celebrities told them to be here. The rest of humanity is sitting on the sidelines. They're not protesting, not voting, not contacting their representatives, not even taking the time to read a one-page article about a global climate crisis that threatens to wash away thousands of years of cultural evolution and millions of years of biological evolution in the span of a few generations. These are the people you want to design and redesign whole societies?"

Her face set into a look of firm determination.

"Yes."

The Preceptor laughed. "Sarah, my dear, you are a remarkable specimen. If the world were filled with remarkable specimens like you, there would be no need for men like me. But the majority of people in this world are simply not capable of determining their own destiny. They must be carefully guided through a rigorous program of conscious evolution spanning several centuries. Trying to make that shift in a matter of months is an incredible act of hubris."

"Hubris?" Sarah laughed. "Seriously? You're going to accuse me of hubris? You're the one who wants to control the future of all of humanity. I just want them to be able to determine their own destiny."

"You know what that destiny is? Death."

The Preceptor raised the gun to his own temple, placing his finger on the trigger. After staring unflinchingly into Sarah's eyes for several long breaths, he pointed the gun at the center of her forehead. As she felt the cool steel pressing against her skin, she eyed his trigger finger warily.

"You've forced my hand, Sarah. You've chosen to fight the system, and the system has chosen to fight back. The Sovereign of the Council of Order has ordered me to shut down the Eutopia Engine and launch a draconian purge of all Anomalies. He and his wealthy allies would rather take their chances with climate change than let the future of humanity fall into the hands of the masses. But as you and I both know, inaction on climate change will cause a global collapse. And so, as the powerful few and the powerless many fight for the right to determine humanity's future, the world will burn."

The Preceptor slid his gun back into its holster. His intuition and the weary look on her face told him that despite her apparent bravado, she felt a similar sense of despair and desperation about their prospects for a successful resolution of the climate crisis. Even without access to the many scenarios and analyses available to him as Preceptor of Order, Sarah had clearly developed an intuitive sense of what he already knew -- that the world was in the process of crashing and burning, and only some highly Anomalous twist of fate would be enough to avert a global catastrophe. He felt a dizzying buzz throughout his whole body as the momentum of history and the potential for change hung heavy in the air all around them.

Suddenly, something shifted in Sarah's expression.

"This Sovereign you mentioned. He's in this building, isn't he?"

The Preceptor felt a great sense of relief wash over him. It was like the tangible shift in the air after a storm breaks, or the feeling of diving into a cool lake on a hot summer day.

Something was changing. His intuition told him that some key element of the Favorable Anomalies scenario was unfolding. What was possible for Order and for humanity was starting to change right before his eyes. And just as he had long suspected, Sarah Athraigh was the key.

The Preceptor smirked.

"I'm not allowed to disclose the location or identity of the Sovereign."

"Right. You are, however, allowed to let Congresswoman O'Neill and guests attend the climate change conference. Unless, of course, this Sovereign of yours intends to publicly capture or kill a member of Congress."

"I'm in charge of security at this event. However, while we've been having this little chat, Homeland Security has declared the Eutopia Engine to be a terrorist plot by virtue of its associations with a newly listed terrorist group called Anomalous Revolution. If Congresswoman O'Neill delivers a public statement supporting the demands of the Eutopia Assembly, she will be arrested on the spot for treason."

"Maybe. But in the meantime, she will be telling the world what really happened at the Eutopia Assembly. And she will be proposing dramatic action by world leaders in response to climate change. And while I'm in there, I'll have a word with your Sovereign about how he and his buddies are refusing to take action on climate change."

The Preceptor took a step forward, leaning in closer to whisper in Sarah's ear.

"You're playing a dangerous game, Sarah." He slid his gun out of its holster, pressing it into Sarah's palm. "Be careful."

Sarah nodded. The Preceptor turned to face his soldiers with open arms and a broad smile.

"Alright! Gentlemen, these people will be escorting this delegate to the conference. Let them through."

Two of the Champions stepped aside, making room for Sarah and her companions to pass through to the main entrance of the building.

"Thank you."

Sarah smiled, turning to motion for her companions to come forward.

"It's alright. They're going to let us in."

Sarah's companions all breathed a collective sigh of relief. Taliesin the healer, Patricia the computer wizard, Hart the costumed superhero, Jonny the rock star, and Congresswoman Irene O'Neill all walked slowly forward, eyeing the Preceptor warily as they passed him. Patricia stuck her tongue out at him, and Hart glared at him, but they all walked past without incident. Sarah joined them, moving to the front of the group and leading the way into the building.

As soon as Sarah and her companions were inside the convention center, the Preceptor directed the police to resume their positions at the barricade. Once the area was secure, he unmuted his connection to the Guardian and checked his tablet for any updates.

The tactical map showed that all major disturbances between Eutopia Assembly and the Garden had been resolved.

"Bill, how's the raid going?"

"Everything's under control here at Javits. We've got most of the detainees on a few police buses and two Order vans full of high-value targets."

"Good."

"And what about the Garden? Looks like you plugged the breach in the barricade."

"Yes. Only the delegates and their parties made it through. There were no major interruptions of the climate conference or disruptions at Penn Station."

"Good. Anything else?"

"That's all for now, Bill. Stay in touch."

"Will do."

The Preceptor breathed a sigh of relief. Now all that was

left to do was to wait and see what Sarah Athraigh's delegation accomplished at the International Conference on Climate Economics.

CHAPTER 22

Every room in Madison Square Garden was filled with three loud, long blares followed by a recorded voice with a British accent speaking over loudspeakers and intercoms throughout the building.

"Attention! Please move to the nearest exit in a calm and orderly fashion. This is not a drill."

The Preceptor looked around the foyer and ticketing area of Madison Square Garden as people attending the International Conference on Climate Economics stopped what they were doing and listened to the announcement. After a few seconds, everyone started gathering up their belongings or moving to the nearest exit. Many of them pulled out their phones and started messaging or talking as they walked. Others were being rushed along in small clusters by what appeared to be the security details of various governmental or corporate dignitaries attending the conference.

Seeing no obvious threat, the Preceptor pulled out his tablet and zoomed in on the Garden. The alarm had apparently been triggered by Garden staff in response to a threat alert from Homeland Security.

The Preceptor unmuted his connection to the Guardian.

"Bill, did you trigger this alert at the Garden?"

"No. I was about to ask you the same thing. How's everything look over there?"

"All clear so far aside from the evacuation. Contact our people at Homeland Security about it. Maybe someone phoned in a threat. I'm going to head up to the convention floor."

The Preceptor motioned for his security detail to follow

him to the main arena where the bulk of the convention delegates and attendees were gathered. They didn't get very far before a sudden surge of panicked people fleeing the main arena slowed their progress almost to a dead stop.

"Push through!"

The Preceptor's thirty-six Champions stepped into a tight arrowhead formation. Each of them pulled a long, clear bar from their belts. They flicked their wrists almost in unison, opening up the collapsible clear riot shields. With shields and rifles in hand, they were able to push through the crowd at a steady jog, deflecting some of the fleeing civilians with shield bashes as necessary.

When the Preceptor and his Champions emerged into the main arena, it was almost empty. Hundreds of chairs, tables, banners, and seemingly random bits of clothing, papers, and equipment were scattered around the convention floor in disarray. Several bodies were lying motionless near the exits. There were also several wounded people on stage, and a cluster of Champions of Order near the stage regrouping and marching toward one of the exits.

As the Preceptor marched into the room, he called out.

"Halt! Initiates of Order, I command you to halt!"

The Champions paused, stopping in place and turning to face the Preceptor. One of them started walking toward him slowly, rifle at low ready.

"Sir, the Sovereign--"

"Halt! The Sovereign isn't here right now. I'm assuming command of his entire detail. Stand where you are and give me a report. Twenty words or less."

"The Sovereign's wounded. He's pursuing an Anomaly. We intend to follow and provide support."

The Preceptor looked back over at the stage. The wounded all appeared to be Sarah's companions, minus Sarah. They were all alive, but all had gunshot wounds.

"Oh, I bet he's pursuing an Anomaly. I'll worry about the Sovereign. Go fetch some medics and police, then return here and guard these people with your lives until I say otherwise."

"But sir, the Sovereign--"

The Preceptor raised his fist in the air. All thirty-six of his Champions raised their rifles and took aim at the Sovereign's Champions.

"Do as I say or you'll be found out of Order. Right here, right now. Am I clear?"

"Yes, Preceptor."

"Then get to it. I'll leave a few of my men here to supervise. For the Victory of Order."

"For the Victory of Order."

The Preceptor motioned for six of his Champions to stay in the main arena and attend to the wounded. The rest followed him out of the main arena through the nearest exit. Before going any farther, he paused, stopping in place and closing his eyes to tune in to his Preceptor's intuition in search of some sign of where the Sovereign had fled to. He immediately felt a rush of utter terror, followed by a hollow numbness.

Something had happened to the Sovereign.

The Preceptor clutched at his chest and gasped for breath, overwhelmed by the echoes of whatever terrifying thoughts had been racing through the Sovereign's mind in his final moments. As he struggled to regain his composure, the Preceptor realized that whatever had happened, it was the last thing the Sovereign would experience.

The Sovereign of Order was dead.

The Preceptor's pulse quickened and mind raced as he struggled to decide what to do next. He muted his connection with the Guardian and pulled out his tablet, opening a video chat with the Insight. As soon as the chat was open, he found himself walking toward the Theater.

"Kendra, I need your help."

"Are you alright, Truman?"

"For the moment. The Sovereign's gone rogue, though. I'm almost at his location, and my intuition tells me I'm already too late."

"Too late? In what sense?"

"I'll get to that in a minute, once it's confirmed. In the meantime--" The Preceptor hesitated, searching for words. "I need you to check something for me."

"Yes. Anything."

"Check out all of the video feeds for Madison Square Garden. Security cameras, livestreams, anything that may have captured the past twenty minutes of chaos, and anything that may still be capturing video. See what we've got and send me a report." He paused. "It would be a shame if some rogue Anomalous element erased all of that data before we reviewed it."

The Insight's eyes widened.

"Yes, I... I think I understand. I'll... look into that right away."

"Thank you."

"Is that all, Truman? Let me know if there's anything else I can do to help."

"That's it for now, Kendra, I'll be in touch soon. For the Victory of Order."

"For the Victory of Order."

When the Preceptor reached the Theater, he motioned for his security detail to wait out.

The Theater at Madison Square Garden was in almost as much disarray as the main arena had been. The seats were stationary, so they were still in place. Everything else -- jackets, signs, papers, even some expensive-looking computers and audio-visual equipment -- had been scattered haphazardly across the chairs and in the aisles.

As the Preceptor walked into the dimly lit room, there were only two people in sight.

Percival Sword, Sovereign of Order, lay lifeless in a pool of blood at the center of the stage. The massive screen behind him shone with the bright colors and bold text of a live feed from PEN News, bathing the stage in a mix of light and shadows that danced across the Sovereign's body. The audio was silent, but the video displayed images from the events unfolding at the

Javits Center and Madison Square Garden: demonstrators clashing with riot police, teargas and stun grenades bursting through the air, strange flashes of electricity and bursts of flame wreaking havoc on buildings and cars and fleeing people. The video was framed by a large block of text declaring "TERROR IN NYC" with the subtitle "ANOMALOUS REVOLUTION TO BLAME".

Sarah Athraigh sat on the edge of the stage, wiping tears from her eyes. The gun that the Preceptor had handed Sarah on her way into the building was lying on the ground next to the Sovereign's body. When she heard his footsteps at the entrance to the Theater, a look of panic flashed across her face. Before the Preceptor could say anything, Sarah bolted to her feet and darted off into the shadows backstage.

The Preceptor motioned for his security detail to follow him into the room. He drew one of his remaining guns and approached the stage slowly, looking around to make sure that there wasn't anyone hiding in the dimly lit room. When he reached the stage, he walked up onto it and examined the body,

The Sovereign was almost unrecognizable. His face was contorted in a look of terror, and his body was riddled with numerous bullet holes, including one to the left temple. The flickering light of the PEN News video feed on the massive screen at the back of the stage cast sharp, irregular, moving shadows across and around his motionless frame.

The Preceptor sighed. He holstered his weapon and motioned for his security detail to approach him. Once they were all within earshot, he cleared his throat and spoke.

"The Sovereign of Order has fallen. I need to have a private conversation with the Guardian of Order about this immediately. Guard the body and don't let anyone near it who's not from Order."

"Yes, Preceptor. For the Victory of Order."

"For the Victory of Order."

The Preceptor walked off the stage and into the shadows backstage. There was no sign of Sarah Athraigh, or anyone else for that matter. After taking another quick glance around to see if anyone was listening, he pulled out his tablet and opened a video chat with the Insight.

"He's dead, Kendra."

"The Sovereign?"

"Yes."

The Insight sighed, shaking her head.

"How did it happen?"

"Multiple gunshot wounds. But it was something more than that." He paused, searching for words. "Between the look on his face and what my intuition's telling me, I'd say he picked a fight with the wrong Anomaly."

The Insight nodded. "Was it--"

"We may never know, Kendra. There's been a lot of chaos here. Breaches of the barricades, stampedes, an active shooter on the main convention floor. We may never know what exactly happened here today. And the video feeds?"

The Insight paused. "It's just as you feared. Some Anomalous faction tampered with the video feeds."

"Thank you for the update, Kendra. I need to talk to the Guardian now."

"Good luck."

"Thank you. For the Victory of Order."

"For the Victory of Order."

The Preceptor closed the connection and put away his tablet. He unmuted his connection to the Guardian and looked back out at the body lying on the stage.

"Bill, I've got some bad news."

CHAPTER 23

The Preceptor's black helicopter descended swiftly from the overcast sky, landing almost silently at the center of the cobblestone helipad at Providence Catalysis. He emerged from the helicopter wearing the same clothes he had worn to his Preceptor initiation: a tailored wool and silk black suit and a golden sash with a bold embroidered black "O" with a white center.

As the helicopter departed, he walked down the cobblestone path that led to the main entrance of the red brick building. Four life-sized marble archangel statues were kneeling on either side of the path, their hands clasped in prayer and their heads bowed in deference to those who passed between them. The Preceptor paused a moment under their gaze, studying the masterful sculpting and looking down at the simple but elegant cobblestone path that held their undivided attention.

Eventually, he headed into the building.

The Preceptor rode in silence down the slow-moving freight elevator that led to the massive hidden Cold War-era bunker that was home to the Inner Temple of Order. He walked alone down the long, cold concrete corridor that led to the ten-foot cube room where his ceremonial garb was waiting for him. The garb he now wore while serving as Preceptor was similar to what he had worn for his Preceptor initiation, but with the main color scheme reversed: a black knee-length tabard with gold trim and a large white "O" on the chest along with a simple black belt with a gold buckle and trim.

As he put the tabard on over his suit, he idly wondered if this would be the last time that he would ever wear it. Once he was fully dressed for the occasion, he waited for the sound of the bell, and proceeded into the next room.

The Inner Temple of Order was a large round room with a smooth marble floor and domed marble ceiling. There was also a large marble altar at the center of the room. As expected, there were only thirteen other people present.

The Council of Order sat in thirteen golden thrones arranged in a semicircle facing the heavy oak doors at the entrance to the room. They were dressed in ornate black robes adorned with various sashes, hoods, cords, and medallions. For security reasons, they were almost never in the same physical location at the same time. The only exception to this rule was for Level 5 initiations and Council initiations. For this reason, he had been called to appear before the Council immediately following the initiation of the new Sovereign of Order.

As the Preceptor walked down the red carpet and approached the altar, the Councillors studied him in silence. When he reached the end of the carpet, he fell to one knee, bowed his head, and awaited the approach of the new Sovereign of Order, Hylda Wyndham.

Hylda Wyndham was a middle-aged woman with brilliant blue eyes, a sharp Roman nose, pale skin, and chin-length hair that was an even blend of black and grey. Her presence was every bit as commanding as that of the previous Sovereign, if not more so. Whereas Percival had broadcast his presence loudly and assertively with every word and gesture, Hylda's understated and solemn demeanour conveyed a certain poise, prudence, and quiet strength. She wore a solid diamond crown emblazoned with a large diamond Eye of Providence framed in a gold circle over the center of her forehead.

When the new Sovereign reached the altar, she motioned for the Preceptor to stand.

"Welcome, Preceptor of Order. Rise and stand before the Council of Order."

The Preceptor rose to his feet. The new Sovereign walked back to her throne at the center of the Council of Order and took a seat. She allowed the silence to linger for a moment before continuing.

"You have been summoned here today to respond to the Council's questions about the various Anomalous incidents that transpired during and after Order's raid on the Eutopia Assembly. This includes the unfortunate loss of the previous Sovereign of Order. Do you have anything to add to your written report?"

"No, Sovereign. I stand ready to answer any questions you may have about the incident."

"Good. You spoke of your prior knowledge of the Percival Sword's Anomalous ability to influence minds. We have reviewed the matter and concluded that he did, in fact, possess such an ability."

The Preceptor breathed a sigh of relief. His greatest concern about the Council's summons was that they wouldn't believe him about this ability. The new Sovereign raised a hand as if to interrupt the Preceptor's moment at ease.

"However, we do question your decision to keep this information from the Council prior to his death. Why did you do so?"

"I suspected that the Council may be under his influence." He paused, considering his words carefully. "I also suspected that even if you weren't, you wouldn't take the claim seriously, and would see it as a power play in response to our disagreement about the Favorable Anomalies scenario."

One of the Councillors snorted and sneered at the Preceptor's remark. The new Sovereign raised a hand to silence the interruption.

"We'll get to that in a moment. Rest assured, however, that the Council of Order is resistant to all mind effects. The Egregore of Order provides this protection to us, as it does to you in your role as Preceptor. All Initiates of Order are graced with a trace of this resistance, but only we possess it in full. In the future, do not assume that our integrity has been compromised, either by Anomalous abilities or by our partisan stances on matters of Order policy."

The Preceptor bowed slightly.

"Of course, Sovereign."

"And then there is the matter of this dispute of yours with the Sovereign. Your Favorable Anomalies scenario versus his Consolidate and Rightsize scenario."

"Yes. Under his scenario--"

The new Sovereign raised a hand to silence the Preceptor.

"We on the Council are well acquainted with the implications of both scenarios. Our earlier pronouncement on the subject, which the previous Sovereign conveyed to you on several occasions, still stands. You are hereby instructed to accept as a matter of settled Order policy the proposition that allowing or overseeing the rapid depopulation of the human species may be necessary for the good of Order. Do you understand this pronouncement, and accept it as binding on all action you take in your role as Preceptor of Order?"

The Preceptor felt his chest tighten and pulse quicken at the thought. He took a deep breath and bowed slightly in assent to the new Sovereign's statement.

"I do, Sovereign."

Several members of the Council, including the new Sovereign, nodded approvingly. The Preceptor thought he heard at least one of them breathe a sigh of relief.

"Good. Very good. In light of recent events, I would like to clarify that unlike you and the previous Sovereign, we on the Council do not have a partisan bias toward either scenario. Humanity may emerge from this global crisis with ten billion members, or it may be reduced to six-hundred and twenty-five million members. Or it may find a new point of balance somewhere in between. We are indifferent to the details. What we care about most is that all is in Order -- that human civilization remains relatively stable, that development proceeds in the intended direction, and that Order itself endures and flourishes so that we may guide humanity through the coming changes. You are instructed to pursue whichever scenario seems most likely to achieve this end, regardless of population and other factors. Do I make myself clear?"

The Preceptor bowed slightly.

"Yes, Sovereign."

"Good. We have one last question, then."

The new Sovereign looked around at her fellow Councillors for a moment. A silence lingered in the air that seemed to grow in weight the longer it lasted. Eventually, the new Sovereign spoke.

"Some on the Council are concerned that you may have orchestrated the death of the Percival Sword. Given your knowledge of his Anomalous ability and your well-known disagreement with him on key matters of Order policy, you had a clear motive. Given your unorthodox alliances with Anomalous factions, and your presence at the site of his death, you would have opportunity. However, if you are to continue in your role as Preceptor, we must come to clarity on this matter. Did you, in fact, orchestrate the death of Percival Sword?"

The Preceptor hesitated. This was the question that he had most feared. However, that also meant that it was the question he was most prepared to answer. He took a deep breath, let it out slowly, and responded in a calm, confident tone.

"That is a question I've been asking myself ever since the moment I found him. No, I did not orchestrate the death of Percival Sword. However, I didn't prevent it either. His plan to implement a public purge of all Anomalies placed him at great risk of Anomalous reprisals. I took no additional action to protect him. In a sense, then, I allowed this to happen on my watch. But I had no specific knowledge of any plans to assassinate him, and did not in that sense orchestrate his death."

There was a rumble of quiet conversation among the members of the Council. The new Sovereign spoke quietly to the Councillor to her right for a moment, then raised her hand to silence all side conversations.

"The Council will deliberate in closed session to discuss the appropriate consequences for your actions in this matter.

Given the fact that your intentions were to preserve Order rather than disrupt it, I expect you will retain your role as Preceptor. However, we may place certain specific limits on your authority as Preceptor, either temporarily or permanently. You must take no further action that would endanger any Councillor or Level 5 Initiate in any way. And from this moment forward, your contact with any Anomalous factions must be supervised directly by either the Guardian or the Catalyst. Do you I make myself clear?"

"Yes, Sovereign."

"Do you agree to these terms?"

"Yes, Sovereign."

"Very well. We will contact you via secure channels with the details of our decision. In the meantime, unless you have any other questions, you are free to leave."

"Thank you, Sovereign. For the Victory of Order."

"For the Victory of Order."

The Preceptor bowed fully and turned to leave. After taking a step toward the door, however, he paused, turning to face the Council of Order.

"Actually, I do have one question."

"We will hear your question, Preceptor. Speak it now."

"Does the Council of Order agree with the assessment of my staff and our metamodel projections that catastrophic climate change is the single greatest threat facing Order at the present time?"

Someone on the Council snorted and sneered again. The new Sovereign raised a hand to silence the interruption.

"We do not have unanimous agreement on that point, Preceptor. However, we do have a majority in agreement. All but one agree that it is a serious concern, and more than half agree that it is currently our greatest threat. The recent death of a Sovereign of Order over this matter has served to underscore the potential it has to destabilize all of Order. One way or another, we must resolve this global crisis -- and very soon. Does that answer your question, Preceptor?"

"Yes, Sovereign, it does. For the Victory of Order."
"For the Victory of Order."

CHAPTER 24

The Preceptor and the Insight walked together along the shore at the Insight's waterfront property in Iceland. The Preceptor was once again struck by the sharp contrasts of color and texture on the beach -- the flowing cerulean waves crashing against the hard black sands of the rocky shoreline, the white foam and mist blurring the line between land and ocean, the crystal blue sky peeking through dark clouds, the Insight's flame-red hair standing out against the black of her coat and the shades of blue and black all around her. The air was filled with the strong scent of saltwater and wet sand, and the wind was even stronger than usual, pulling at their hair and coats in sudden gusts. From time to time, the howl of the wind across the rocks and the crash of the waves on the shore made conversation difficult -- but if they leaned in close and spoke up, they could still hear each other.

"So that's the end of their investigation into Percival's death, then."

"Yes." The Preceptor breathed a sigh of relief. "At least officially, anyway. I get the impression that there are at least one or more Councillors who are dissatisfied with the outcome. But I am still Preceptor, and the limits they've placed upon my authority so far have been reasonable, if a bit cumbersome."

"Good. And what about Athraigh? Did the Council mention her?"

"No. Honestly, I don't know if they're aware of her role in Percival's death. They didn't ask, and I didn't tell. They know that Anomalous forces were responsible, but may not know the details. If they do, they're not taking action against her."

"And what about you? Will you be taking any action against her?"

"No."

The Preceptor stopped, staring out across the ocean. The Insight stopped alongside him, waiting for him to continue.

"The Favorable Anomalies scenario is still our best bet. And Sarah Athraigh still seems to be playing a central role in it. Ever since she came on the scene, the projected success rate of Favorable Anomalies has increased significantly. And the success rate of Percival's Consolidate and Rightsize has started declining. Clearly, Favorable Anomalies is the way forward."

"And yet, the actual state of the world as reported by our metamodel has been in steady decline since Athraigh's arrival on the scene."

The Preceptor sighed.

"Yes. The Eutopia Engine has already destabilized society to some extent, just as we feared. And the raids on the Eutopia Assembly and other Anomalous sites have only made it worse. The public now knows far more about the existence of the Anomalous than they used to. The consequences of that revelation have been complex and largely negative. A lot of people are researching the Anomalous now and joining underground movements to create social change, including a rise in Anomalous Revolution recruitment that may soon replenish the large number that we managed to capture in the raids. But to be fair, the integrity of consensus reality was already in decline anyway. That's what started us down this whole path of pursuing the Favorable Anomalies scenario. It's just all happening faster than we anticipated."

The Insight nodded. "As is the onset of catastrophic climate change."

"Yes."

The Preceptor and the Insight started walking along the shore again. They walked together in silence for several minutes before the Insight spoke.

"What's your next move, Truman? I've been doing a lot

of analysis of recent events and how they affect the various scenarios. Favorable Anomalies is the option with the highest chance of creating a favorable outcome for Order and the world generally. But by its very nature, it leaves us without much guidance on what our next action steps should be. With Favorable Anomalies, we just sort of cross our fingers and hope that the favorable Anomalous factors at play work out in our favor. So… what do we do?"

The Preceptor stopped. He stared out across the ocean, watching the waves crash against the shore and contemplating what his next move should be. Eventually, he spoke.

"I don't know, Kendra. I don't know."

ABOUT THE AUTHOR

My name is Treesong. I'm a father, husband, author, talk radio host, and Real Life Superhero. I live in Carbondale, Southern Illinois. I write novels, short stories, and poetry, mostly about the climate.

Learn about my other books, poetry, and Real Life Superhero adventures on my website (treesong.org), Facebook (@TreesongRLSH), or Twitter (@Treesong).

OTHER BOOKS BY TREESONG

CHANGE
See Order through the eyes of Sarah Athraigh!

What does global warming look like in a world full of magic, superheroes, and secret societies?

Sarah Athraigh, an environmental activist from Southern Illinois, stumbles into the midst of a hidden war between occult factions that are grappling with the root causes and dire consequences of climate change. As she goes on the run, she soon finds herself on a journey of discovery, searching for the unusual allies and innovative ideas that will help her to respond to the looming threat of catastrophic climate change.

Change is a contemporary fantasy tale featuring a strong female lead, superheroes, secret societies, modern magic, political protests, the power of music, and a colorful cast of characters that Sarah meets along the way as she searches for solutions to the climate crisis.

GOODBYE MIAMI
Tales of An American Climate Refugee

What happens when global warming turns Americans into refugees? Kass, an American climate refugee, flees Miami in the wake of a hurricane that leaves most of the city underwater. After moving in with her cousin in Southern Illinois, Kass struggles to deal with her displacement. She hopes to find a way to return to the city that she loves. But thanks to global warming, that city is now underwater. What starts as a search for survival soon evolves into a struggle for the future of Miami -- and the world.

Goodbye Miami is a dystopian political thriller featuring a strong female lead, climate refugees, political protests, community organizing, and creative solutions to the challenges of grassroots climate adaptation in a major city that has succumbed to catastrophic flooding.

CLI-FI PLUS

Cli-Fi Plus is a climate fiction anthology with an emphasis on genre and theme crossovers. Each short story combines elements of cli-fi with elements of more established genres and themes in sci-fi and literary fiction. The result is an entertaining read that keeps you on the edge of your seat and leaves you wondering what will come next in the real-life climate crisis.

What does a cli-fi alien story look like? What does a cli-fi robot story look like? What does a cli-fi zombie story look like? What does a cli-fi time travel story look like? What does a cli-fi political thriller look like? What does literary cli-fi look like? Find the answers to these questions and more in Cli-Fi Plus!

READ MORE OF TREESONG'S FICTION AND POETRY
AND LEARN ABOUT HIS SUPERHERO ADVENTURES
AT TREESONG.ORG

www.ingramcontent.com/pod-product-compliance
Lightning Source LLC
Chambersburg PA
CBHW022143240626
47153CB00007B/2487